Dear Papa

Dear Papa

ANNE YLVISAKER

CANDLEWICK PRESS
CAMBRIDGE, MASSACHUSETTS

Copyright © 2002 by Anne Ylvisaker

First edition 2002

Library of Congress Cataloging-in-Publication Data
Ylvisaker, Anne.
Dear Papa / Anne Ylvisaker. — 1st ed.
p.   cm.
Summary: In September of 1943, one year after her father's
death, nine-year-old Isabelle begins writing him letters, which
are interspersed with letters to other members of her family,
relating important events in her life and how she feels about them.
ISBN 0-7636-1618-4
[1. Letters — Fiction.   2. Fathers and daughters — Fiction.
3. Family life — Minnesota — Fiction.   4. World War,
1939–1945 — United States — Fiction.
5. Minnesota — Fiction.]   I. Title.
PZ7.Y57 De 2002
[Fic] — dc21   2001037608

2 4 6 8 10 9 7 5 3 1

Printed in the United States of America

This book was typeset in Goudy.

Candlewick Press
2067 Massachusetts Avenue
Cambridge, Massachusetts 02140

visit us at www.candlewick.com

For
Elisabeth Thomas,
who pointed me in a new direction,
and
Judy Delton,
who taught me how to read the map

❖1943❖

Dear Papa,

Today in school we are learning proper letter-writing form. We are supposed to write to someone we haven't seen in a long time. Tomorrow it will be one year since you went to heaven, so I picked you. Notice that each new idea gets indented for a new paragraph.

A lot has changed on Palace. The Christiansons moved and the new family doesn't have any children of their own really, but they have a big man that plays hopscotch on the sidewalk. He thinks he's six but I know he's not.

The awning blew off the south window in a storm last summer and Mama said if you aren't coming back to fix it, well, we just don't need that awning. So I guess the sofa will fade.

Now we end with a salutation. I don't know what to write on the envelope. Miss Lockey gave us each a stamp. I'll use Aunt Izzy's address. I know she was your favorite sister.

Sincerely,

Isabelle

Dear Papa,

Boy, was Aunt Izzy surprised to get your letter. But she didn't tell Mama and I think she's my
favorite of your sisters, too. She wrote back and
said I can send a letter to you anytime, but I only
had the one stamp and we've moved on to writing poems in school.

Mama bought me another notebook but said
no more writing after 8 P.M. That's when I have the
best ideas, I told her. I am a night owl, like you.

I don't have an envelope so I will put this
in my Bible since that's the nearest address to
heaven I can think of.

From,
Isabelle

October 24, 1943

Dear Papa,

Remember the people in Christiansons'
house, with the man who plays hopscotch? Their
name is Jordahl and you wouldn't know it from

their name but they are Catholic! And what is more, they bought your filling station! The day after my last letter, Mama was crying for you. She went through three hankies with the five of us plus Irma's boyfriend watching. All in a sudden, she stopped, stood up, and declared that enough was enough. It was time to get on with things. She called up Mr. Jordahl because he's been asking what Mama's going to do about the station, as it hasn't been run very well without you. And she said, fine, Mr. Jordahl, you can buy that station and take over as soon as you can.

Now where will I get my ice cream? Stanley, who's been running everything, always let me pick something out of the case, but I don't think I can ask a Catholic man for ice cream just because it used to be my father's station and I used to help out scrubbing the counter and straightening the shelves. In addition to that, the boy-man helps out Mr. Jordahl. If you ask me, I think he will scare off the customers with his hopscotching in the parking lot, but you didn't ask me. I miss you asking me, Papa. Things like, How was your day, lollipop? And, Where's the fire, chief? And now I forgot to indent. It will be a wonder if I can pass one more grade without a father.

　　With fondest regards,
　　Isabelle, age nine

Dear Papa,

　　It is Halloween. I am dressing up as you! I found your old coveralls with the NILS patch and I stitched up the legs with a needle and thread. Now let Irma say I'm hopeless with sewing! I'm going to say "fill 'er up" instead of "trick or treat"! What do you think of that? Irma and Inez have to stay here and answer the door and Mama is walking around the block with us younger ones.

　　Back to Palace and things that have changed. Charlie the cat ran away and now that makes no more pets: three dead fish, one run-over dog, and two runaway cats.

　　Boo-hoo!
　　Isabelle

Dear Papa,

Mama got a job! I hope you don't turn over in your grave like she says. We all tried to eat a little less but that doesn't pay the electric bill, she says. It was expensive for you to go to the hospital, and then to be buried besides really added up. (Not that we blame you!) Mama is working at five different houses, one every day except Saturday and Sunday. She cleans each house all in a day. Little Ida goes with her. In the evenings she figures the books for Mr. Jordahl. I think she's tired.

Remember when she was tired that other time, after Ida was born and you just put us all in the back of your truck and drove around all day so she could rest? We went across every bridge in the city, just to count them. I was afraid one of us, especially me, would bump out and into the Mighty Mississippi.

Inez has a boyfriend now, too. His name is Charlie (like the cat!). He is very handsome and helped Mama put the awning back up. He's handy with things. Irma's boyfriend (remember Stuart?) joined the service and is trying to talk Charlie into joining, too. Inez and Irma are very proud. Little Ida isn't so little anymore. She doesn't remember you much, I'm sorry to say. Ian is just plain mad to be left with us females. We don't roughhouse like you did. Charlie and Stuart knock him about for play, though.

Mama has me bring the books to Mr. Jordahl at the station and who is still there helping out but Stanley! I do get an ice cream after all. But I'd rather have you there chinging the register and not have any ice cream at all.

Fondly,

Isabelle

November 22, 1943

Dear Papa,

You wouldn't know Mama now, I think. Even if you did come back, which I guess you won't. Her smiles are gone and there's no time for holding little Ida on her lap. Mama's voice isn't cinnamon brown anymore. It is sharp red or tired gray. I wrote a story for school yesterday called "The Inventor of Colors." You were the inventor, Papa.

Do you get to sleep in heaven and if so do you have dreams and if so do you dream about us like we dream about you? Last night I dreamed you made me toast. But it burned up like the time you made breakfast for Mama on her birthday.

This week is Thanksgiving. Irma and Inez want to make the whole meal to impress the you-know-whos. (They want Mama to invite over their families.)

Your pumpkin pie,
Isabelle

Dear Papa,

It is Thanksgiving Day and Mama won't get out of bed! We none of us know what to do. She got up last Thanksgiving, which wasn't so long after your funeral. We had turkey then and everyone had something to report being thankful for. But this morning when I went downstairs, the teakettle was cold. Mama and I always are the first ones in the kitchen in the morning. She warms the kettle and I talk, which she says is how she gets her dose of daily news. Well, not only was the kettle cold, but Irma and Inez were in the kitchen arguing about whose crust is the flakiest. Charlie and Stuart can't come for dinner, but they are coming for pie. "Where's Mama?" I asked. "Not down here," Irma said.

I went up to Mama's and your room. She was breathing, thanks be to God. But she was way down under the covers and rolled over away from me when I came to sit on the bed. She had a picture of you in her hand. "He sure was handsome," I said, and she started crying! Our Mama crying! Can you imagine? "I'm lonely for him, too, Mama." I said. Sob sob sob and more sobbing. "Mama, he was handsome, but he's dead," I said. Then she rolled over. "Isabelle," she said, "your sisters know how to get the bird in the oven. Go help them. I'm so tired."

I went down and told the girls about Mama and the turkey. They both went tripping up the stairs even though I said she wanted to rest.

So now you are up to date. Uncle Bernard

always tells me I need to be a soldier. To be strong for Mama. But I can't lift that turkey by myself.

Your girl,

Isabelle

Thanksgiving, later

Dear Papa,

Here we are at the other end of the day. I am thankful because Mama did get out of bed and the crust was flaky and the boys did come over. Here is what happened: Irma and Inez went to Mama. They were in there for a long time. I heard Ida and Ian upstairs hollering so I went up and we cut out paper dolls with a daddy one for Ian. He'll only play if we make some boy ones. I sat real close to the wall trying to hear what was going on with Mama but I couldn't. Finally, Irma and Inez came in and said we should get dressed. We did. Then they said we should eat oatmeal. We did. Then they said we should go outside and play. We did, but it was pea-pickin' cold. And what is the use of cold if there isn't any snow?

We went by Christiansons' where the Jordahls live. That boy-man was looking at us from the upstairs window. Ida waved and he smiled and then he was gone. Pretty soon he came out the front door! He hopped down his front walk in three big hops. He stopped at the end and waved both hands like fluttering birds up by his ears. Ida giggled and I poked her. I don't think we should laugh at him. "What's your name?" I asked him. "Jimmy Jimmy Jimmy," he said. "Want to hop some scotch?" Well, we did. And wouldn't you know Jimmy won? He must have had a lot of practice because he is really good. But he didn't like waiting for his turn. We ended up making two hopscotch plans so he could use one and we could use the other.

Mrs. Jordahl came out and asked us if we wanted to come in. I wonder if she knows we're Lutheran. Anyhow, we did go in. Catholics have Thanksgiving, too, so their house smelled really good. Turns out the Jordahls moved here from Wisconsin and they didn't have anyone coming for dinner. A whole turkey just for the three of them. Mrs. Jordahl asked about our plans. I said I thought we'd be doing Thanksgiving tomorrow, when Mama gets up. She took out the biggest jar of cookies you ever saw and sat us down at the table with Jimmy, and then swept herself right out of the house. We didn't know where she went. After cookies, Jimmy showed us all the rooms. He talks loud. We pretended to be interested even though we'd been there about every other day when Christiansons lived there.

When Mrs. Jordahl came back, she said she'd been to our house and that Mama had invited them for dinner! Mrs. Jordahl called to Mr. Jordahl, who lifted the turkey out of the oven still pink, and we all walked in a parade to our house behind a half-done turkey!

Mama had a dress on when we got there and an apron. She and Inez and Irma and Mrs. Jordahl bumped around each other in the kitchen, getting things done.

Mr. Jordahl sat in your chair and everyone told about a Thanksgiving they remembered. Mama told about you coming out to the farm when you and she were courting. Then she let me have seconds on pie.

Since it wasn't Sunday, only a holiday, Mr.

Jordahl thought it would be all right to play cards, so we did.

Your ace of hearts,
Isabelle

December 7, 1943

Dear Papa,

We sat for one minute in silence at school today. The Japs bombed Pearl Harbor two years ago today, when I was seven. You held me on your lap while we listened to the radio. It was the only time I ever heard you pray except at the table. Miss Lockey says we must all do our part for the duration. I will pray just like you did:

Christ Almighty!

God, damn them all to hell.

Holy Jesus, preserve us.

Mama was so happy to hear you praying, she turned off the radio and asked you to go to church with her right then that night.

In remembrance,
Isabelle

❖1944❖

January 1, 1944

Dear Papa,

It is a brand-new year. I have made some resolutions: Help the first time Mama asks. Hang up my clothes before bed. Go to church with a willing heart. Keep our family together.

Your daughter,
Isabelle, nine and a half today

P. S. (That means there's more to say.) You might be wondering about that last one. Christmas wasn't too good this year. That old Uncle Bernard came driving up on Christmas Eve, right during meatballs and minutes away from presents. Mama made a fuss for her big brother, of course. She pulled up your chair for him at the table. They sat talking and talking and this is what I heard: The family doesn't think Mama should be caring for five children and working every day, too. Mama said she was managing on her income just fine, thank you very much. Well, old U. B. leaned back in your chair (damaging the legs, I'm sure, because he is on the stout side, you'll recall) and then he leaned closer to Mama and said, "Sophie, money is not exactly what I had in mind." That was when Mama shooed us all off to the kitchen to clean up. Ida dropped her plate and Ian whined about presents and Irma wouldn't let me stand close enough to hear what they said next.

I know you aren't supposed to have any troubles in heaven and I hope Jesus doesn't mind if I worry you a bit, but just so you know, nothing has happened yet. I'm only telling you that something is wrong around here and I am trying to find out what it is. I'll write again sooner this time.

January 1, 1944

Dear Aunt Izzy,

Welcome to 1944! You said I could write anytime. How is Muffin? I hope he hasn't gotten stuck in the tree again. The firemen sure came fast last time.

I am writing to you because I need help. Mama won't let me call you. To update you since

Papa died, our cat ran away, Mama went to work, Irma and Inez got boyfriends, and Mama's brother Bernard thinks Mama should send me and Irma and Inez to live with the uncles so her money can stretch farther and her energy, too. Uncle Edgar needs help on the farm and Uncle Bernard and Aunt Jaye want a girl around the house. She just called a family meeting to tell us. She said it is only for a while, but I think that is too long, especially since I am scheduled to go to Bernard's house. They don't have even one child and they have lots of money and a Pontiac. What would Mama do without me to take the electric bill downtown on the streetcar and keep Ida and Ian entertained after school? Irma and Inez would get to go together to Uncle Edgar's farm and they are boo-hooing because they don't want to leave their boyfriends.

So I am asking you please, as Papa's sister, to come here and straighten things out. I know that if Mama had more rest or more money she wouldn't be listening to those brothers. We live at 1234 Palace and you can have my bed when you come. I will wash the sheets today and will be watching for you from the porch window if you come soon enough and I am not already gone.

Your niece and namesake,

Isabelle Valborg Anderson

Dear Aunt Izzy,

It must be a really long drive from California and I'm sure you had to try to get time off work and you would have come right away if you could have. But if you are not already on the road, here is my new address: 1175 Grandview, Zumbrota, Minnesota. (The view is not as grand as the name might suggest. From my window I see right into the window of the nosy girl next door.) The uncles move fast. By the time school started back after New Year's, I was in my new school. My notebooks and pencils and that lovely bookmark you sent for my last birthday are all in my old classroom with my old friends and the best teacher I ever had. Mama promised me that Ian would get them for me, but you know Ian. (Well,

I guess you don't really, but he is the family for-
getter, and besides, he is only six.)

Please consider our dilemma. Children should
be with their mothers, no matter how much
money their uncles have. I know Mama would
listen to you, as you were Papa's favorite sister
and the only one still living. Your siblings sure all
died young. I hope you don't.

From the third-floor bedroom,
Isabelle Valborg

P. S. Did you ever tell any of your friends what
your middle name is? I haven't.

January 16, 1944

Dear Papa,

I am in Zumbrota. Remember when we
came here for the Fourth of July family reunion?
Well, now I am living here. I am not going to put
my clothes in the dresser like Aunt Jaye says
because I do think that Mama will be coming
back to get me this weekend. If it does not snow

too much more, she said she and Ida and Ian would come to celebrate Mama's birthday here. I'm sure she will see by now that it is more work to have me gone than at home. There is a picture here of Mama when she was younger. She had on this little beaded hat and such a big smile. Her eyes were dancing. Was it you she was looking at? In the mirror I think I look a little like that Mama.

Love,
Isabelle

January 17, 1944

Dear Ian,

I have my own room here. Imagine! A bed big enough for two at least, a dresser, a little desk where I am sitting right now, and a window where I can spy on the girl next door. She is ten but thinks she is much older than me. She thinks I am an orphan and doesn't believe that I have any brothers and sisters at all! Just wait until you show up this weekend and she sees how all us kids look alike as paper dolls, just different sizes. We'll see who's an orphan then! Her name is Eleanor, after the president's wife. See if you can think of something we can do to scare the liver out of her when you come!

Is Ida still as stubborn as always? Don't you dare put her in the closet when you two fight, now. And hold her hand during blackouts. Remember, she is the baby of the family. Please write me a letter if you can. Or you could draw a picture.

Have you gotten all my things from Miss Lockey's room yet?

Your sister,

Isabelle

(Hi, Mama! I know you are reading this to Ian. I tried to write big so he could read some of it. Maybe he could just look for all the "I"s or something. Aunt Jaye gave me a whole sheet of stamps. I am enclosing some for all of you. Can't wait to see you!)

Dear Ida,

How is everything in the yellow bedroom? I made you a paper doll. It is me! Can you tell by the straight yellow hair and blue eyes? If we made an Ida doll, we'd need to make lots of curls for her. Can you cut out some clothes for paper Isabelle? I think she'll need a snowsuit. Shoes, too. There is no shoe ration for paper dolls so make her as many as you want.

Don't forget Mama's birthday's coming up. You and Ian could make a card together. (Mama, try to forget this!) I will see you this weekend! You can stay with me in my green bedroom.

Love and kisses,

Belle

January 18, 1944

Dear Irma and Inez,

Thank you for writing. No, I am not adjusting to small-town life. How is everything on the farm? Have you heard from the boys yet? Mama and Ian and Ida are coming down for Mama's birthday this weekend. Are you going to come, too? I am sure Uncle Edgar would bring you since there will be a party with cake, and I remember that at the reunion he ate the whole flag part of the cake. Are you happy being at the farm? I guess you want to get back to the city and Charlie and Stuart and all your friends. Well, me, too. We could work on a plan this weekend.

Uncle Bernard and Aunt Jaye are pretty quiet people. U. B. goes off to the bank every morning and A. J. generally pads around the house picking up and searching for dust. She has given me lots of paper and had this room all ready for me. It should have everything a girl needs, she said. There's even a desk, which is where I am sitting right now. When I moved the chair away from the desk, there were deep dents in the rug.

School was canceled here most of last week because of the snow. So I have only had one day in my new class. I have met the girl next door, though. Eleanor. She is a piece of work, as Papa would say.

From,

Isabelle

January 21, 1944

Dear Mama,

Happy Birthday! I know I heard your voice on the phone just this morning, but it wasn't enough of a chat. I know you don't have time to write but I hope you don't mind getting letters anyhow. I'm glad you and Ian and Ida had pancakes today. Aunt Jaye made them here in honor of your birthday even though you couldn't come. She and I made a cake yesterday. Then the snow started.

Mama, I even made a frosting sewing machine on the cake for you. Aunt Jaye and Uncle Bernard are good to me. I help out like you said, and I try to be grateful. But this house is so quiet. Even the streets are quieter. There is no streetcar. There's only one filling station and I've only been by it, not inside. It is smaller than ours.

I went outside and started making a snow family this morning. I'm going youngest to oldest. I can see Snow Ida out the window and she is growing taller because it is still snowing.

Happy Birthday to You! Happy Birthday to You! Happy Birthday, Dear Mama! Happy Birthday to You!

Love,
Isabelle

January 22, 1944

Dear Papa,

Yesterday was a sad and happy day. Sad because Mama called to say she couldn't come because there was too much snow. Happy because later, who should come banging on the door and stomping snow onto Aunt Jaye's clean rug but Irma and Inez! Uncle Edgar's truck made it through the snow from the farm. We had a big time. We finished the snow family in the backyard that I had started in the morning. We made you taller than Mama even though you weren't really. Uncle Bernard gave us a hat for you and we used a big pickle for your nose! I waved up at the window of the girl next door (Eleanor). But I don't think she saw us.

Then we went inside and ate up Mama's whole birthday cake and played cards by the fire. Irma has a new hairdo. She looks like a college girl. Inez brought me a book to read.

They left a little bit ago. We plumb forgot to talk about a plan for getting back home. It's too quiet now. I can hear U. B. turning the pages of his newspaper downstairs. I need to braid Ida's hair or pester Inez or race Ian to the corner and back. Most of all I need Mama to wrap me up in her arms and kiss the top of my head.

Aunt Jaye is calling again. I would have gone the first time if it were Mama's voice calling.

I.V.A.

Dear Papa,

I got a letter from Jimmy Jordahl! It was all pictures with a note from Mrs. Jordahl saying Jimmy asked about me and that Mama is doing just fine and Ian and Ida go to her house sometimes to play. Jimmy draws really good. He drew two sides of a paper full of hockey players. I could tell what they were with no writing at all. I'm going to write back and draw something for Jimmy and ask about your station. I wonder if they've changed the name. I heard Stanley talking about it once with Mr. Jordahl. I think your faithful customers would be disappointed.

Bye!

Isabelle

Dear Papa,

I have been to school here for three weeks now. I have to walk to school with Eleanor. All she does is talk, talk, talk. Her daddy this, her daddy that. Her mother is the head of all the Red Cross activities for the greater Zumbrota area, including all the farms. Eleanor takes piano lessons and has given a recital that the mayor himself attended. I told her that my daddy was in oil but she didn't believe me. She doesn't believe much so I have started giving her some good stories to disbelieve. She's reading *The Secret Garden* and I think that secretly she wishes she were an orphan like she thinks I am.

This afternoon when we walked home, Aunt Jaye was out on the front porch waving at us as we came up the street. She dashed down the walk and said that Eleanor's mother was out so Eleanor should come in for a while. Oh, Papa. If it wasn't bad enough that I had to listen to her all the way home, which was long, by the way, because people hadn't shoveled their walks yet and we had to trudge through snow up past our boots, then to have to sit at the table and share cookies and milk with her. Ugh. Aunt Jaye was chatty for a change and asked Eleanor all kinds of questions, which made her talk even more. Then A. J. suggested I take Eleanor up to my room and find something to play. Eleanor had to be in charge of everything — what game we would play (Parcheesi), who would go first (Eleanor), whether blockades were allowed or not (only when Eleanor was blocking me, it seemed!). I thought her mother would never rescue me. Fortunately, I have really good luck at Parcheesi and Eleanor was very ready to leave when we heard the door open.

From,
Isabelle

February 15, 1944

Dear Aunt Izzy,

Thank you for the new bookmark. I am reading *The Secret Garden* and have marked the page I am on. I am glad you have written to Mama. I can't wait until you come out this summer. What is "Crafty Ladies" that you said you go to on Wednesdays? If it is crafts like knitting, what do you make? If it is witchcraft, write right away because I can't wait to tell Eleanor next door that I have an aunt that's a witch! And if you are, does that mean that I might be, too?

I am sorry to hear about Muffin. Some trees are just too tall.

From,
Isabelle

February 16, 1944

Dear Papa,

We just ate dinner, Uncle Bernard and Aunt Jaye and me. The table is so big and it is all shiny with no fingerprints. They talk in quiet voices, and I know I should be grateful that they are helping out Mama this way. But I don't want me not being home to be a help to Mama. Aunt Jaye likes to braid my hair and she bought me a new blue dress and she sits on my bed while I'm at my desk and waits for me to talk to her. But 1234 Palace is where I want to be.

From Zumbrota,
Isabelle

Dear Papa,

When I can't go to sleep at night, I imagine I'm walking through our whole house. Inside the porch door are all sizes of coats on hooks and off of hooks and shoes in a jumble. Mama's shoes always stand at attention at the left side of the door, the toes touching the wall.

"Teach me numbers!" Ida says to Ian.

"Mama, keep her away from my model airplane," Ian wails.

"Way down upon the Swanee River..." Irma and Inez practice their songs for choir.

Creak, crack, creak, crack, Mama's rocking chair goes back and forth over that place where you glued the rockers back together. In my mind I imagine she is knitting a pink sweater for me and she's dropping it on the floor and jumping up to hug me when I walk in the door. I put you in the

31

pictures, too. The back door slams and Mama puts her hands on her hips. Then you come around the corner grinning big and wiping grease off your hands onto your pants before you pick me up and twirl me around.

Sometimes I wish I could go to sleep and wake up when I was seven and things were like they used to be.

In loving memory,
Isabelle

Dear Papa,

Mama and Ian and Ida are here today! Mama's been saving the gas stamps from way back at her birthday. We are having what Uncle Bernard calls The Thaw. He says we get one every February. Irma and Inez are coming later. Charlie and Stuart picked up Mama and the kids in Stuart's Ford and drove them here. Then they left to get the girls at Uncle Edgar's. They aren't either one good with maps because Mama had to be firm about where to turn to get here, she said, but I am sure they will return victorious.

Mama and Ian and Ida are all resting after the long drive, but I can't sleep in the middle of the day.

Bye!

Is

February 21, 1944

Papa,

I know you probably thought this letter would come from Palace but it is not. I thought it would, too. In fact, I don't think I'll write to you tonight after all. If you had been here, you would have made sure I was in that car when it turned around for St. Paul. I shouldn't talk to my own father like this but I'm mad at you for leaving us.

I. Valborg

P. S. I'm glad you named me after Aunt Izzy but couldn't you have given me a beautiful middle name like Meredith or Betty?

Dear Papa,

I'm sorry I wasn't nice in my last letter. I know you didn't die on purpose. I wish you were here to send me to my room for back talk. Aunt Jaye and Uncle Bernard never punish me. They think everything I do is cute. I'm nine and more than a half for pity's sake!

I want to tell you about Mama's visit. It was so wonderful the first day. She hugged and hugged and hugged me. She did my hair and talked to me like she used to. She looked happy, Papa. Really. The girls came and the house was noisy and Ian and Ida and me made a big mess in my room with all the toys Aunt Jaye keeps in there. We ate sandwiches for lunch and played whist around the big table. I heard Mama laugh. Later we all went on a walk to the downtown of Zumbrota. Uncle Bernard opened up the bank even though it was a Saturday and gave us a tour. Charlie had to carry Ida most of the way, but he didn't mind. Ian and Ida and I slept in my room and Mama sat in there until we were all asleep. I slept all night without one dream.

In the morning we all got spit and polished for church. We took up a whole pew. Afterward we had roast and potatoes and Mama was different again. The brightness in her eyes and voice was gone and she crabbed at Ian when he dropped a biscuit on the floor. Then she just got up and put on her coat to leave.

"Mama," I said. "I want to come home."

"Isabelle, don't make this harder than it already is."

"Mama," I said again. "I want to come home!" And then I started bawling like a big baby. Mama didn't come and wipe my tears off or ask me to quit crying. She just stood there like a woodcarving.

"Isabelle, pull yourself together," Irma said.

"Irma!" Inez said, and she came and tried to wipe off my tears but that made them come faster.

"Girls, don't fight," Mama said in a bigger voice than I've heard her use in a long time. She got up and hugged each of us, but it was like an uncle hug, not a mother hug. Then she went out to the car and Irma buttoned up Ida and Ian and they all piled on laps and left.

Since Mama is working all the time, the girls are away, and you're dead, it looks like it's up to me to solve the problem. Mama will be so proud.

Love,
Isabelle

March 1, 1944

Dear Aunt Izzy,

I am anxiously awaiting your reply about Crafty Ladies. I have enclosed an envelope with my address and a stamp on it. Good news: I am going to go home and so are Inez and Irma to finish out their senior year. Bad news: I don't know how, yet. But I am working on it. Here's what we know so far:

1. Mama needs time and money.

2. Uncle Bernard and Aunt Jaye need someone to take care of.

3. Uncle Edgar needs help on the farm.

4. Isabelle and Irma and Inez need to go home.

Here's what I've done so far:

1. Wrote a list.

2. Started a prayer chain. They have them at the church here. It is not a paper chain, but a people chain from what I gather. Pastor Porter says God answers every single prayer, just ask. I don't know a lot of people here to put on the chain, but I called Eleanor over. It was the best I could do. I set her to work praying for the things on the list. "When you get to the end of the list, just start over at number one and do it again," I told her.

"If I'm going to pray, I need atmosphere," she said.

She ran over to her house and came back with a Bible, a candle, and a lace hanky and set them up in a corner of my room. It looks pretty Catholic to me, but at least she's praying.

I'll let you know what happens.

Isabelle

Dear Aunt Izzy,

I've added some things to the plan.

3. Adopted bad habits. Aunt Jaye has lots of advice for me. One thing she says is, "Good people, good habits. Bad people, bad habits. Surround yourself with good people, Isabelle, and you will adopt good habits. Take Eleanor for example," and then she is off and running. Well, I can't help being around Eleanor, but if I have bad habits, Aunt Jaye will not want to have me here, I am sure of it. So I have worked on learning to burp like Papa did after dinner sometimes when Mama was out of the room. I put my elbows on the table, chew with my mouth open, and slouch. Tomorrow I am going to say "darn." I couldn't think of any other bad habits but I am studying the kids at school, particularly LeRoy Pence, as he has no manners at all.

4. Here is where you come in. If you know of any spells that could help with any of the above situations, please send detailed instructions.

Your crafty niece,

Isabelle

Dear Papa,

I am hoping that if I adopt bad habits, Aunt Jaye will give up on me and send me home. Being bad is turning out to be not so hard as I thought it would be. And I'm wondering, Papa, am I bad? Is that why Mama doesn't want me? Was I very bad when you were here?

Here's what I did today: Aunt Jaye made me oatmeal for breakfast, which was really very nice because it was cold this morning. But as you may not know, because of the war even rich people can't buy all the sugar they want. So there was no sugar for my oatmeal. I said, "I'm not going to eat this darn mush without sugar! It's sour like everything else at this darn funeral home." It just popped right out of my mouth like I'd been saying it every day. Uncle Bernard dropped his spoon and got oatmeal on his tie and he said, "Damn!"

Oh, my. I thought Aunt Jaye was going to faint or choke on her own breath. My eyes got all wet like they were going to cry but I remembered

Mama and stuck to my plan. I swished my hair back like I saw Eleanor do before she back-talked her mother and just walked away from the table. I stomped on the stairs and slammed my door. All this in less than five minutes. The trouble was that when I got to my room, I didn't feel like I was acting anymore. I unmade my bed and took yesterday's clothes back out of the wardrobe and threw them on the floor.

Pretty soon there was a big rap on the door.

"Young lady, there is no excuse for your behavior. You go downstairs and apologize to your Aunt Jaye this minute. I want a good report when I get back from the bank." Uncle Bernard didn't open the door, but I heard him breathing his loud fat man's breathing out there on the landing for a whole minute before he left. After I heard him leave the house, I did go downstairs. Aunt Jaye was still standing at the sink holding the dishtowel. I said, "I'm sorry I complained about the bad food." She didn't even look at me. I put on my coat and boots and left for school a half-hour early and without Eleanor.

Miss Jensen, my new teacher, let me come in

and sit at my desk. I was going to give up on the being bad idea, but then LeRoy Pence pulled my hair on his way into the classroom and Sue Joan Warick asked why I didn't have a mother or father, and I hit her. I really did, Papa. What kind of example will I be for Ian and Ida if I do go home?

With a contrite heart,
Isabelle

March 11, 1944

Dear Papa,

It is Saturday and I am supposed to stay in my room all day because of yesterday. Uncle Bernard and Aunt Jaye, not having much experience with bad children, are not sure what to do with me. I heard them arguing about it last night. Aunt Jaye called Eleanor's mother and this is the punishment she recommended. What they don't know is that this isn't punishment at all. In my room alone I don't have to try to be good or bad. I have my whole day planned out. I am going to write to you and Jimmy Jordahl and Aunt Izzy.

I won't write to Ida and Ian until I know I can be a good example. Then I am going to pretend I am an orphan and this is the turret at the top of the abandoned castle where they keep orphans. I will rearrange the furniture and draw pictures to hang on the walls. I will spy on Eleanor out my window. Plus, I have the rest of *The Secret Garden* to read. Mary's parents didn't love her and they died. I wonder if she will get happy in the end.

I'll probably write later, since I have all day.

From,

Isabelle

March 11, 1944

Dear Jimmy,

How are you? What is new? Could you please draw me some more pictures? I will hang them on the wall in my room. I have to stay in here all day. What do you do all day at home? I have never seen you go anywhere except the station. Did you ever go to school? Say hi to Stanley at the station for me.

Here are some pictures of the people and places in Zumbrota. Hopscotch is popular here, too.

Your friend and former neighbor,
Isabelle

March 11, 1944

Dear Aunt Izzy,

Your letter arrived today! It made me so happy because I am being punished today and cannot leave my room. Aunt Jaye brought your letter up with my lunch. I was disappointed to read that Crafty Ladies is crafts after all. I'm sure the soldiers appreciate the scarves you knit, though. No, I don't know how to knit. I have enough time for handwork, I guess. I have been saving toothpaste tubes for the war effort. Do you get the comic *Little Orphan Annie?* Annie says kids can help the war by collecting scrap metal.

Remember the plan I sent you? It is not going too well. The bad habits part kind of took off. I am not sure how to stop. Now instead of

Aunt Jaye giving up on me and sending me home, she seems almost happy. She is walking around the house faster and talking in a firmer voice than usual.

"Isabelle," she said, "you've been allowed to be too free here. Children need a purpose and it is my job as your current guardian to give you one." She went on, *blah blah blah*, about the projects we'll get involved in at church and the chores I will take over at the house. I'm afraid I stuck out my tongue at her when she bent down to pick up some lint off the floor.

Every day I pray, "Dear Father in Heaven, thank you for this day. Please take me home to my mother." Maybe I should have had more people on the prayer chain. Maybe God hasn't checked the prayers in Zumbrota lately. He'd get more prayers per block by going to St. Paul where there are churches on every other corner and there are houses on both sides of the river. I wonder if Jimmy prays. He's got the time for sure.

Isabelle

Dear Mama,

How are you? I am fine. I am reading the Bible today like you said in your note I should, and catching up on my letter writing. Did you know that Jesus left his parents for a while? They thought he was bad because they couldn't find him. But when they did find him, they discovered that he had been talking with people at the church, which is a good thing. So his parents took him home.

Did you take the electric bill downtown? I do miss running errands for you. I like being your helper. Aunt Jaye finds me a great help here. I am now in charge of all the dusting, turning the crank on the clothes wringer, drying the dishes, and sweeping the porch. That last one will start when the snow melts. I am enclosing a sample of my schoolwork. Could you have Ian bring it in to Miss Lockey? I want her to see that I am keeping up so I'll fit right in when I come back. By the way, Mama, when will that be? Just so Miss Lockey can have my desk ready.

Aunt Jaye is calling. I am always ready to help the first time she asks. When I come home, I will come the first time you call, too.

Your obedient daughter,
Isabelle

March 11, 1944

Dear Irma and Inez,

We could surprise Mama and be home for Easter. Invite Uncle Edgar for dinner and maybe he'll drive our bags and us in his truck. We should be living on Palace by now. If we don't get there soon, maybe Mama will get used to life without us. You two could help her after school at the houses she cleans and I could watch Ida and Ian and we'd be a family again. Please respond quickly.

From,
Isabelle

Dear Papa,

My day of punishment is almost at an end. I did get to eat supper downstairs. But things have changed. Uncle Bernard and Aunt Jaye watch me like a bug in Ian's pickle jar. Every time I think I will fly like my old self, I smack my face into the glass.

At dinner, after he finished his boiled potatoes, Uncle Bernard wiped his wide chin and said, "So, Miss Isabelle, how did you spend your hours today?"

I thought about it and told him the part I knew he would most approve of. "I read my Bible quite a lot."

Aunt Jaye snorted. I heard her!

"Isabelle," U. B. said, "this is not a hard question. I highly doubt you were up there reading the Bible. Let's start again. How did you spend your hours today?"

Why didn't they believe me, Papa?

"I read about Jesus going to the temple and his parents couldn't find him but he was only talking to the older people there and I was thinking that was kind of like me being here with you, and then his parents came and took him home and soon my mother will come and take me home."

Well, that made him mad. He went on about blasphemy and me comparing myself to Jesus (which I wasn't), and them being old people was offensive and wasn't I just the ungrateful one and didn't I learn anything at all being in my room all day. My head boiled, I was so mad. But I did not do a thing to show it. You would have been proud. I just sat there eating my horrid peas. Every one I smooshed in my mouth I imagined was U. B.'s head. After a bit of considering he asked Aunt Jaye what she had planned for my Sabbath. Papa, it includes embroidery! I am supposed to embroider dishtowels for the newcomer baskets. For one thing, how many people can be moving to this town with a war on, and for another, I hate embroidery. It is slow and dull and I'll probably doze off and the needle will pierce my eye when my head falls. Life can be complicated. It makes me tired.

Good night.

Isabelle

Dear Irma and Inez,

    1. I got your letter today after school. Charlie and Stuart are gone? I was hoping the war would be over before they would have to go.

    2. How could you possibly *like* life on the farm? Pigs live there and cows, and I know how you both hate bad smells. You say you feel so grown-up running everything and not having to answer to Mother, but she is our mother! We are a family! I am checking your handwriting very closely because I think maybe Uncle Edgar wrote this because he wants you to stay and take care of the house for him. What about your friends? What about school? What about ME?!

    3. If you aren't here on Good Friday, I will go home without you.

    With sincere disappointment and disgust,
    Isabelle

March 22, 1944

To Irma and Inez:

I will so go by myself. Miss Jensen has a map at school. Every inch is ten miles. Zumbrota is six inches from the middle of St. Paul, which is about where Palace must be. Miss Jensen says people usually walk between three and four miles an hour, though she didn't care to time me. So it would be 25 hours at least to get home. Can you think of your small sister (well, her legs are pretty long and her arms do hang down low, but still . . .) walking all of Good Friday and into Holy Saturday? All by herself? And can you imagine her arriving home to her mother's rhubarb pie and eating her sisters' pieces because her sisters aren't there?

Have you mentioned anything to Uncle Edgar yet?

Waiting for a reply,
Isabelle

To Irma and Inez,

I was going to give you a day or two to write and a day for the mail to make the short trip from Uncle Edgar's farm, but I must move ahead with my planning in case I cannot depend on you. I found out that we could take the bus home. It leaves Fridays at 2:00 in the afternoon. It stops in downtown St. Paul and I know how to get the streetcar from there. I am going to be on that bus on Good Friday. Are you? A few things need to be worked out before then:

1. Money. Do you have any? It would be $1.50 for one of us (me), $3.00 for two, and $4.50 for the entire family to be reunited. (If you can't agree, at least one of you could come. Inez, remember what you told me once about Irma bossing you? Don't fight because I told.) A bargain when you think about it. I have 63¢. But don't worry. I will come up with my own fare.

2. Secrecy. I am assuming that the uncles would not agree to us going home. It is Lent, and though it is always wrong to lie, I am even more

nervous about it during Lent. So let's don't lie, exactly. I'm thinking that if I don't say to Aunt Jaye and Uncle Bernard I am going or am not going, it is not a lie to just go.

3. Luggage. I'll have to leave as if for a walk to the library, so I think I will only be taking my book bag.

4. Have you thought about how you will get from the farm to town that day? This is your problem to solve, along with luggage and money.

That is all for now.

Isabelle

March 27, 1944

Dear Papa,

I'm not so fond of school as I used to be. Yesterday LeRoy Pence found out his dad was killed in the war. He didn't come to school today. Miss Jensen told us about it. No one likes LeRoy Pence much because he doesn't seem to like anyone else much, except that big dog that scared the socks off me when it followed him to school on Valentine's Day. But now his father is dead. I never met him, of course, but when Miss Jensen told us about it, I started to cry. In class! I was so mad at myself. That made me cry harder. Eleanor said on the way home that I shouldn't feel bad because LeRoy's dad was mean anyhow and nobody liked him much. But I do feel bad. Bad all over again. Now in a couple weeks Jesus is going to die again, too.

Well, as mother says, enough is enough. So now I am going to make a list for my trip home. I am planning it with Irma and Inez, but have not heard back from them. I think I'll close with a picture this time. It will be you and me building the birdhouse we made for Mama when I was six. We both hammered our thumbs and you pretended to cry as loud as me. So turn over the page. Or can you see through paper?

Love,
Isabelle

March 28, 1944

Dear Papa,

Only ten days until I go home. I opened my window when I woke up and saw a spot of ground through the snow. I think there will be an early spring.

LeRoy Pence came back to school. He didn't pull my hair even though I stopped right in front of him in line to give him the chance.

I looked around my classroom today at the people I won't be seeing anymore. There will be an even number again for kickball.

I wonder what Mama will say when she sees me?

Love,
Isabelle

Dear Papa,
Just waiting.
Isabelle

Dear Papa,

Aunt Jaye hugged me today. She told me how happy it makes her to hear my feet pounding down the stairs in the morning.

"I'm so proud of your work for the newcomer baskets. Your embroidery is quite fine," she said.

Mama would like a towel, I think. I will stitch all our names on it. Even yours.

Yours in stitches (ha-ha!),
Isabelle

Dear Papa,

I am invited to Eleanor's birthday party. She invited every girl in our class. There is going to be a real cake. Her mother's been saving sugar. Aunt Jaye is making me a new dress, but I won't be wearing it. The party is after Easter and I won't be here. But I stood on the stool anyhow and let A. J. measure me.

Your much-taller-than-last-year girl,
Isabelle

Five days left

Dear Papa,

I took three dollars out of Aunt Jaye's sewing box. She thinks thieves won't find her money there if they break in. I saw it under the spools when she measured me. I wonder if Uncle Bernard knows that she does not support his bank with her money. I need money for the bus. I am praying for forgiveness, but I am not giving the money back. If you see Jesus around there, will you please explain? I know he's busy with Holy Week and such and probably didn't even notice, but I'd like to clear this up right away.

I went to Eleanor's after school today. She has this catalog full of clothes and toys. She gets to pick birthday presents out of it. She had thirteen things circled! There was a set of doll dishes I sure would like to get for Ida. I can't wait to comb her curly yellow hair and fold her little white socks.

Love,

Isabelle

April 2, 1944

Dear Mrs. Jordahl,

Thank you for sending Jimmy's pictures. Please ask him about the one with the family on it. It looks like Ida and Ian and my mom. But there is a man in the picture. Who is it?

Please reply quickly.

Your neighbor,

Isabelle

April 2, 1944

Dear Irma and Inez,

 All right. I'll go alone.

 Isabelle

April 3, 1944

Dear Aunt Izzy,

 Thank you for the postcard. Do you really have flowers in the winter? I would love to taste an orange from your yard.

 You can send any future mail to 1234 Palace. I am going home on Friday. It is kind of a surprise.

 Why does your trip out here depend on the war? There's been war since I can remember. We did see you that once. Was there war then? Why did you move so far away from the place you grew up? Did you travel to California by yourself? Can you tell me about my mama and my papa from the old days? I'll send along an extra sheet of paper for your reply. I have a lot of paper left here and I won't be able to take it all with me. Maybe Aunt Jaye will take up writing after I leave.

Love,
Isabelle

Three days until home

Dear Papa,

Today when Aunt Jaye hugged me, I hugged her back. Uncle Bernard doesn't hug or I might have almost hugged him, too. I am so excited to go home that I feel like being good. I helped clean up the dishes without a fuss. I didn't hiss at the squirrels looking for nuts in the backyard. I even picked up Sue Joan Warick's pencil when it dropped on the floor. She may remember that act of charity next week and feel sad that she didn't get to know me better. "Where did that Isabelle girl go?" she'll ask Miss Jensen. "I was going to invite her to my birthday party." I'll be somewhere better than a party.

This room on the third floor has been nice. But I like the closeness of the walls in my room on Palace and little Ida breathing loud through her mouth all night long.

Eleanor has been over here quite often. When Aunt Jaye feels the need to have a girl around again, she can call on Eleanor.

Good night, Papa!
Isabelle

Maundy Thursday

Dear Irma and Inez,

Was this our Last Supper tonight, like in the Bible?

When you came with Uncle Edgar for dinner today, I thought you were in on my plan. I waited up until . . . well, until now, and it is 10:32 P.M. I snuck downstairs and unlocked the back door because I thought you didn't really leave with U. E. but were going to creep back and join me. I thought we'd have the whole ride home to talk so I didn't tell you about everything during dinner.

What has happened to the two of you? I don't know you anymore.

Thank you for the package. I don't know if I can get everything in my book bag, though. I will at least bring the cloth doll you made for Ida and the cap for Ian. The pencil for me will fit for sure.

You didn't tell Uncle Edgar, did you?

Goodbye (forever?),

Isabelle

The Day Before Home, 11:00 P.M.

Dear Papa,

Irma and Inez are one big disappointment. They were here today. But even though they know Mama would feel better having us home, they are not going back with me. I know you are their father so you have to love them, but you must be mad at least for them leaving me alone like this.

I am too nervous and excited and scared and happy to sleep. There are three books here I have not read yet. I think I'll read all night.

I'll write tomorrow from HOME!

Love and kisses and hugs,

Isabelle

Dear Aunt Jaye and Uncle Bernard,

If you are reading this note, then you are standing in my room. Don't have any worries about me. I am fine. I am on my way home, where I should have been all along. Mama needs all her children around her when her spirits are low.

I am very grateful for everything you have done for me. I especially thank you for all the paper.

Aunt Jaye, I'm sorry I won't be able to wear the dress you already started. Bess Hart in my class has never ever had a new dress and she is about my size. Maybe she could wear it to Eleanor's party.

Uncle Bernard, thank you for the extra money it took to feed me. I do eat a lot, like you said. I am sorry I was mouthy about it when you brought it up. I wish you and your bank a lot of success.

Please don't call my mother. I want to surprise her. Maybe you can come for a visit soon. Mama will make a pie.

Your niece,
Isabelle

P. S. There is a note for Eleanor on my desk. Would you please give it to her? I stitched up a towel for her birthday. Not as good as something from the catalog, and I hope you don't mind me taking one from your supply, and thread, too, but could you wrap it and bring it over with the note? I don't want her to open it at the party but beforehand. Another thank you.

April 7, 1944

Dear Eleanor,

Happy Birthday in advance.

Happy Easter, too.

I will not be able to make it to your party, and don't wait for me to walk to school next week. Guess where I am? I'll tell you: By the time you read this I will be home in St. Paul with my little brother and sister and my mother. I will be back in school next week in Miss Lockey's class.

Even though we got off to a bad start and a bad middle, too, you are a good friend. You set up that corner to pray and gave me your dry sock and wore my wet sock when my boot came off in the snow on the way to school.

I hope you can visit me sometime. I live at 1234 Palace. I'll show you the filling station my papa used to own. If you come in August, we could go to the fair.

Your city friend,
Isabelle

P. S. Could you please say goodbye to Miss Jensen for me? I liked it when she read out loud to us. And don't mind LeRoy Pence so much. He doesn't have a father now.

Dear Papa,

I am on the bus with Inez! I never heard of twins splitting before but our pair did. I was buying my ticket at the drugstore and the lady at the counter said, "You're too young to buy a ticket, Miss." And who should walk in the door but Inez. "It's all right. She's with me," Inez said. She bought a ticket, too, and the bus pulled up and took us on board. I was so happy about her being here that I told her about writing to you. She doesn't want to include a note with mine but said to say hi.

I have to take back half of what I said about Irma and Inez. Inez got up before the milking this morning and ran off to town with a boy from the next farm over. He'd agreed to bring Inez when she showed him my letters.

Inez and I have got a lot of catching up to do. I'll write more later.

Your traveler,

Isabelle

Dear Papa,
>Here we are on Palace, but not at 1234.
>Am I an orphan, Papa?
>Too tired to write more.
>*Isabelle*

Dear Papa,

Inez and I are at Jordahls'. We stayed last night in the room next to Jimmy's. He snores. Here is an account of yesterday.

The boy in the seat behind us on the bus threw up before we were even at Cannon Falls. We should have known then to turn around for Zumbrota. But we put hankies over our noses and slept. Found the streetcar in St. Paul. Rode to Cleveland Avenue. Walked home. Knocked on the door. No one home. Sat on the step. Still no one home. Left our bags and walked to Jordahls'.

"Oh, mercy!" said Mrs. Jordahl. "When did you girls arrive? How did you get here?"

"An Easter surprise for Mother," I told her. "We've come home!"

"Have you seen our mother?" Inez asked her.

"Have you talked to any of the other neighbors?" Mrs. Jordahl asked us.

We shook our heads and waited.

Mrs. Jordahl was wearing the same apron she had on at Thanksgiving, when Mama didn't get out of bed. She wiped her hands on it and sat us at the kitchen table. No cookies this time but a good loaf of bread, and traveling does make one hungry.

And I guess why I'm stalling, telling you all the details, Papa, is Mama just isn't home. All you need to know now is that she's living close to here with Ian and Ida and we will see her tonight. But maybe you don't want to know the whole story?

Your Isabelle

Dear Aunt Izzy,

We are a neighborhood scandal.

How will I go back to Miss Lockey's class now, when my mother has left the house my papa bought for us and moved in with a man she cleans for? A bachelor man. A Catholic bachelor man.

I have been in St. Paul only two days and already I have been stared at and whispered about. Mostly at church.

Inez and I got here Friday. We stayed at Jordahls'. Saturday Mama came over for dinner at Jordahls'. Oh, the hugging and kissing! She was so happy to see us. (Not happy enough to rush right over when we got here.) But she was a different Mama. She was dressed up in a new dress and my hands touched each other when they went around her waist. Her hair was young and her giggles were, too. And she had with her the owner of the house, Mr. Francis something-or-another. Mrs. Jordahl told us that Mr. Francis needed live-in help to cook and clean. Mama and the kids have their own part of the house. But live-in help's children should not call the helpee "Papa Frank."

From,

Isabelle

April 11, 1944

Dear Papa,

I was with Mama for Easter like I wanted. Ian and Ida found the most eggs. It was a tie. I didn't look real hard.

Mama had been saving meat stamps, and there was a ham with enough for Inez and me even though we were unexpected guests.

Love,

Isabelle

April 13, 1944

Dear Eleanor,

Hello from St. Paul! Did you wear a new hat for Easter? Only two days until your party. I am sorry I will miss it.

It is wonderful to be in St. Paul again. My family was the center of conversation after church on Sunday. Our previous home was a bit too small for growing children so we have moved to a larger house by the river. My mother kept it as a surprise for my sister Inez and me. What fun it was to pick out a new room. Wish you could see it.

How is everything at school?

Since we have moved, I will be going to a different school than before I left. I will start next week. I am practiced at being the new kid.

Your friend,

Isabelle

Dear Aunt Izzy,

I am fed clear up to my eyebrows with Mama's "Whee! Let's pick out a room at Papa Frank's for you girls," and "Whee! Isn't it clever of you girls to find your way home by yourselves," and "My, my, how you gave your aunt and uncles a fright." I am thinking about calling Pastor Grindahl and telling him that one of his flock was socializing with her boss on the night before Christ was raised from the dead.

How is Inez doing with all of this you may be asking yourself, probably while stroking the fur of that new striped cat of yours. Inez couldn't be happier. Mr. Frank lives on a very nice street called Mississippi River Boulevard, which will be good for her social life. She and Mama yabber it up, making fun of Uncle Edgar's stutter and more that isn't fitting a mother of five, and during wartime, too.

Before I left I took stamps from Uncle Bernard's desk. I guess sin runs in the family.

Please write to me at 1234 Palace. I will check the mail every day even though no one is living there.

Maybe I'll go by Valborg now. I am in an ugly mood.

Sincerely,
Valborg

April 23, 1944

Dear Aunt Izzy,

I guess you are waiting for my new address, as the only mail at Palace has been bills. It is (for now): 2455 Mississippi River Boulevard. There is room for you here for sure. Ida and Ian and I walked through the whole house yesterday and counted the rooms. There are fourteen, including three bathrooms. "Never a line," says Mr. Frank. There are three bedrooms in our part of the house. And a room for nothing but sitting and reading or playing games. One room is Mama's, one for Ida and Ian, and one is now for Inez and me.

I went downstairs the first few mornings I was here to sit in the kitchen with Mama. It is not like the kitchen days on Palace. I feel like a visitor when I sit with my own mother. She is busy but not the stomping busy she was before I went to Zumbrota. She is humming busy, wearing a clean apron and nodding at me when I talk but crossing things off lists and stirring and wiping all the while. It is all right though, as I cannot think of a lot to say.

"Aren't we lucky to live here?" she says to me. She was going to come and get me soon, as soon as she could figure out how Things would work out. "One day you'll understand," she said. But she goes on wiping plates and doesn't notice that I've braided my own hair, when we spent so much time practicing before. I wish I could feel as lucky as Mama.

Isabelle

Dear Aunt Izzy,

It is a long walk to Palace, but Inez and I did it today. We played hopscotch with Jimmy and looked in the windows of 1234. Jimmy had to lift me up. Everything inside the house is waiting. The front porch was open and Mrs. Jordahl let us sit there and eat our snack. Inez wasn't hungry so I ate hers. The paint is rubbed away from the wall where we used to kick off our shoes. Afterward, Mr. Jordahl drove us back to Mr. Frank's. He didn't stay.

We've been in St. Paul for three weeks and I am with Mama and the rest, but I am not home.

What would Papa think of all this?

How do you like your place in California? Maybe you would like to move out here and buy your brother's house. I'd live in it with you. Your new cat would love all the trees around here.

From,

Isabelle

April 30, 1944

Dear Papa,

The lilac buds are coming out. I braided Ida's hair today. Imagine. It took her so long to get hair and now it is long enough for braids.

Mama doesn't have to work so hard now. She only cleans one house. I thought that would make you glad.

Love,
Isabelle

May 1, 1944

Dear Papa,

The truth of the matter is that we are living in the house Mama is cleaning. We are not living on Palace.

From,
Isabelle

Dear Papa,

A man owns the house. He is a Catholic. But we have our own part of the house. It is on Mississippi River Boulevard. We still get gas at your station.

Love,
Isabelle

Dear Aunt Izzy,

Mr. Frank wants to "get to know me better." Pshaw! He has hair growing out of his nose. He did not go to war to fight for this country (on account of he is too old and besides he has a withered-up hand). He drives up to the station and waits in the car while Stanley fills the tank. He does not get out to lean on the car and make conversation like Papa's regular customers did. Instead he shouts jokes out the window in a big tuba voice. He thinks he is funny. I am surprised

Mr. Jordahl will take his credit. I will not call him Papa Frank like Ida and Ian. They are too young to know better. Little Ida is as bouncy as her curls. She would call the milkman Papa if he hung around long enough.

I started a new school. My teacher is old. The children are wild. I skinned my knee on the playground my very first recess. I'm so lonely I even miss Eleanor. And almost Aunt Jaye. I'd miss you if I'd seen you more recently.

Here is a stamp. Please send me a letter.

From,

Isabelle

May 7, 1944

Dear Papa,

There is more to the story. I'm sorry I had to keep it from you and now I can hardly face my pencil when I write to you.

We are living in the house of a bachelor man. Mama cleans his house and cooks. That's why we live here. But I overheard Mrs. Leonard at church talking to Mrs. Jacobson. "It's not right," she said. "Sophie's inviting trouble. That man takes Sophie and the kids around like they are a family and I've heard the little ones call him 'Papa Frank.'" Ida and Ian just don't know better, Papa. I tried talking them out of it but they already have the habit.

Your girl,
Isabelle

May 8, 1944

Dear Aunt Izzy,

I am just wondering. Mama didn't have any sisters of her own, so did you two seem like sisters when she married your brother? When I ask her about you she raises her eyebrows up. Do you like her? Does she listen to you? Will you talk to her? Maybe she just needed someone to talk to and she was here cleaning one day and Mr. Frank listened and she stayed. I'd be happy to look for some money to send you for the long-distance bill if you would call her on the phone. You don't have to say I said to call. I don't think she thinks about Papa enough now. You could send me a picture of my papa that I could accidentally leave out on the mantle. I only have one picture of my papa and I keep it by my bed so I can sleep. Now I can't remember any of his faces except the one he is making in the picture, surprised because he had just pulled his head from under the hood of a car when Stanley snapped a shot with his new Brownie. I know he wasn't always surprised, but I forget the mad face and the silly face and the listening-to-the-radio face. Do you forget his big-brother face?

School was better today. Back in Zumbrota I learned to spell lots of words so I could beat out Sue Joan W. and Eleanor in the spelling bee. Now I know more words than any kid in this class. Today was a spelling test and my new teacher smiled at me. I didn't know she knew how.

I know that despite what Mama says about you, she would like to get a long-distance phone call.

From,
Isabelle

Dear Papa,

You taught me to hold my head high no matter what people say. But today when I stood outside at recess and the Mississippi River Boulevard kids were playing on one side and the rest of the kids were playing on the other, I didn't know where to go. Some kids have said mean things about Mama. I got detention for socking Donald yesterday. Then today the Boulevard kids pretended I was not there when I asked to join kickball, and the other kids argued over who had to have me on their team.

Do you see any Catholics in heaven? Mr. Frank does not live that different from us, except for the big house and nice car. The Jordahls don't either, except for going to church on Saturday sometimes and Jimmy being the way he is, but he would be that way even if he were Lutheran, Mrs. Jordahl says.

Love,
Isabelle

May 11, 1944

Dear Papa,

Ian and Ida are going to draw a picture of you. I thought it would be best if they had some reminders that you are their papa, though you haven't been here in a while. When Mama is busy with what she does around this house, Ida and Ian really listen to me. I tell them stories about you. In fact, I have started to put the stories in a book I made with a stack of paper and fasteners from the desk of Mr. Frank. He has an office somewhere downtown but has an office in the house, too! When I went in there to ask him to please not hold Ida's hand in public, I left with a stack of supplies. He gave them to me, not like the towel and money I took unlawfully in Zumbrota. He recognizes that girls such as me have to look out for their families. He'd been cleaning his desk and wondered if I would be able to make use of some of the supplies that are extras, as no one is supposed to waste during the war (or anytime else, I told him). I have paper clips, fasteners, lined paper and unlined paper, and a box and a scissors. I will do my part for the war effort and put the supplies to good use, I told him. So I am making a book. It is like a history book. My new teacher is big on reading history. She said if *some people* had paid more attention to history, specifically the Great War, we would not be having war again now. Well, if Ida and Ian learn about the history of our family, maybe they will not be so eager to have it all changed up. A few parts I am having to fill in on my own. I know you won't mind. Sometime I'll have Mama or Aunt Izzy check facts for me, but writers must get the words out, my teacher says. She would know. She talks all day.

Yours,
Isabelle

May 12, 1944

Dear Papa,

Ian said today, "Papa never was sick. He just left." I told him he was dead wrong. I saw you in the hospital all puffed up after they gave you that medicine. Then I saw them put the box in the ground after the medicine did not work but blew up your insides. I hope I never get an allergic reaction. But Ian and Ida did not see the box. They had to stay home with the Christiansons. I am putting a chapter in my book called "The Death and Funeral of Mr. Nils Anderson."

It is Friday. We eat fish here every single Friday. I didn't notice until it happened three Fridays in a row, and when I pointed it out to Mama, she said that's what the Catholics do. The smell is bad even when Mama fancies it up with the recipes she's found in the Altar and Rosary Society cookbook. It is her job to cook and clean here so she is only following the rules. I know she would rather be fixing a bacon sandwich for you.

I am putting Ida's picture of you with my letters. She can't be expected to remember your face exactly. I think the fact that she drew you to look like St. Nicholas must mean that she remembers you as a happy papa. I told Ian to start over. He put you hanging off the back of a train leaving town. He must not have understood the assignment. I don't remember you ever taking a train trip.

Stanley said yesterday, "Sure miss your Pop, Isa-bellie-boop." Me, too. I slipped him a twenty-five-cent tip out of the coins Mr. Frank gave me.

Love from,

Isabelle

May 16, 1944

Dear Aunt Izzy,

Mr. Frank took us to the movies Saturday. When we walked in, we saw the Nelsons from the old neighborhood. She never was my mother's friend and her daughter Beverly never was mine. But Mrs. Nelson came right up to Mama and put her hand on her arm.

"Sophie, you look wonderful! And how your children have grown. Why haven't we seen you out in the yard yet this spring?" Here she paused and smiled her red lips at Mr. Frank, then looked back at Mama. "Anything new, dear?" She raised her eyebrows way up and leaned close to Mama when she said it. That's why I never played with Beverly. Always on gossip patrol.

"Nothing I can think of," Mama said. "And you?"

Mrs. Nelson does not give up that easily but Mama just smiled big and fake and turned to walk into the theater. We all scurried to catch up with her but not before Ida had to say in a voice big enough for the whole lobby to hear, "Papa Frank, can we get popcorn?"

"Sure, doll!" he bellowed and grabbed her hand. "How about the rest of you?"

It is like that everywhere. Mr. Frank doesn't go with us to church because of being Catholic, but people talk anyhow.

Mama says Mr. Frank is lonely. That is why we eat at his table at supper. And why he takes us places and stands in the kitchen drying the dishes and talking to Mama after supper. What do you think, Aunt Izzy?

Isabelle

May 17, 1944

Dear Aunt Jaye and Uncle Bernard,

Mama said I gave you quite a fright when I left. I hope I didn't add to the gray hairs Mama says you're sprouting. How are things in Zumbrota? Have there been many newcomers? Are the lilacs blooming? What did you see going on next door on the day of Eleanor's party?

Have you talked to my mother? Did you know we have moved? We are on Mississippi River Boulevard. Mama is the live-in help for Mr. Frank Colletti.

He is a bachelor and Catholic. Just thought you should know.

We would love to have you to dinner next Sunday. Church gets out at 12:00 so dinner could be at 1:00. It should be a nice spring day for a drive, I think. It is a surprise for Mama. We will all be planning on you unless I receive a letter. Maybe you could suggest to Mama that we move back to Palace.

From,
Isabelle

May 17, 1944

Dear Irma,

How is spring planting going? I am no longer so mad as when I talked to you on the phone from Jordahls'. Inez misses you, though. I can tell.

We need to do something about Mama. It is not right that she is living here in sin. We could live on Palace and she could drive to Mississippi River Boulevard. Inez isn't so sure. We have to let Mama be the mother, she says. (Who changed her from melody to harmony, I'd like to know!) Ian and Ida are too little, and since you didn't come home, the least you could do is help out.

Please come to dinner this Sunday at 1:00. Inez and I are going to cook. Uncle Edgar is invited, too, of course. Aunt Jaye and Uncle Bernard will be here. Maybe you could ride together. It is a surprise for Mama.

We'll plan on seeing you unless you write to me first.

Your sister,
Isabelle

May 21, 1944

Dear Papa,

Inez and I made dinner today.

Irma and Aunt Jaye and the uncles were here, too. That part was a surprise for Mama. Mr. Frank is a doctor so he was working. Can't close the hospital like you can (could) the station, I guess. The food turned out good, but there are quite a few leftovers.

Having her brothers here was not such a good surprise for Mama after all. Bernard raised his voice, Edgar stuttered, Mama used a bad word, and Aunt Jaye cried and cried and hugged and hugged me. Irma rolled her eyes and said to Inez, "See why I don't come back?" Then she said something disrespectful about Mama, and Inez slapped her face! Ida wailed for Papa Frank, and Ian just walked out the door and I didn't find him in the tree until almost dark. Would we have been a disappointment to you, if you had been here today?

Inez and I cleaned up the whole dinner. She is thinking about going to college or signing up for training to be a war nurse. She will graduate in a week. Irma will, too, but from a different school.

Love,
Isabelle

May 22, 1944

Dear Aunt Izzy,

Mama is selling our Palace house.

I am afraid it is my fault. Inez's and mine. We should not have invited the uncles for dinner last weekend without telling Mama. What will happen if Mama loses her cleaning job here?

Please think about coming back to your roots. The house is real nice and you and Mrs. Jordahl would be friends, I'm sure.

Mrs. Winthrop back on Palace has a job in the factory that used to make Fords and now makes guns and tanks for the war. Lots of ladies are working there.

You could call here and reverse the charges if you like. Mama has Irma do that every Sunday.

Do you need ration stamps to feed your cat? We're always running low on meat stamps and Mama says Ian and me have hollow legs. When you come, bring your ration stamps.

From,

Isabelle

Dear Aunt Izzy,

Has something happened to you?

Maybe you are sick.

Maybe you have moved.

Maybe you have finally gotten married.

(Why aren't you married?)

If you read this letter, please respond.

Mr. Frank hired a cleaning lady.

She cleans our part of the house, too!

Mama is wearing makeup and is not cleaning.

1234 is still for sale.

Isabelle

June 3, 1944

Dear Papa,

Mama is married.

Of course it is Mr. Frank that Mama is married to. (Or it is Mr. Frank *to whom* Mother is married.) It happened way back in March while I sat in my room in Zumbrota worrying about my Mama. Because of the mixed marriage, they didn't say anything. They married in secret at a courthouse. But after the disaster with her brothers, Mama declared that she was a grown woman and deserved her happiness. I wonder if it was Mr. Frank that made Mama stop feeling tired. She says she was worried about my detentions at school for defending her and that her being married to a man outside the Church was not as bad as being accused of living in sin.

Mr. Frank and Mama sat us all down after supper tonight and told us. Mr. Frank went on about what a great man you had been and how you would always be our true papa, but that he would like us to come to love him, too. And how our mother makes him so happy and we will all be a happy family. It was worse than the gushy movie we saw at the Nile last weekend.

After that Mama got on the phone and called Irma and told her. Then she called up Uncle Bernard and told him.

Don't worry, Papa. I am still your girl. I didn't let Mr. Frank hug me. I didn't call him Papa Frank, except one time when it slipped out during croquet when I won and was too excited to think clearly.

My head is in a spin. Inez and me are going for a walk.

Your very own girl,
Isabelle

June 4, 1944

Dear Papa,

Inez told me I am being a brat. She is glad that at least Mama is talking and cheerful and doesn't have to work. Inez is happy that Mr.

Frank is going to send her to college. She says I am ungrateful.

Do you think I am being ungrateful, Papa?

Love,

Isabelle

June 5, 1944

Dear Papa,

They got married in a courthouse, but now I find out they had a CATHOLIC PRIEST bless their marriage! That way he can still go to church, Mr. Frank says. I asked Mama what priests act like and do they speak English and is the inside of the church anything like the Lutherans' (Catholic churches always look better from the outside, if you ask me) and she said she'd just have to take me there so I could see for myself. That was not what I meant! I think I will have the flu on Sunday.

Don't worry, Mama is still Lutheran.

Your nearly feverish girl,

Isabelle

Dear Aunt Izzy,

Thank you for writing to me at last. I know that you are happy living the way you are and thank you for the list of what is polite to ask and not polite to ask. I was just curious is all, though now that you mention it I can't stop wondering what you weigh, even though that was on the don't-ask list. You were not as big as the other adults when I saw you, I think. But I was only four then and it could be that I remember it that way because you sat with me on the step. I weighed 65 pounds at the start of last term. They took my height and weight at the school in Zumbrota. I wonder if I will be tall like Mama or small like Papa. Right now I am in the middle.

I am afraid your letter to Mama was too late. If she has not already written you back, here is the news: Mama married Mr. Frank. That is why the new cleaning lady. As the wife of Dr. Frank Colletti, she no longer cleans except to pick up after us now and then.

I know you will be disappointed to receive this news. I am, too. But at least Mama's spirits are better.

Poor Papa.

From,

Isabelle

June 9, 1944

Dear Papa,

I am a Stepdaughter. What a dumb word. There is not one other stepdaughter in my class. I'll bet there isn't one in all of Zumbrota or in Miss Lockey's class either.

"Hello, have you met my wife, Sophie?" Mr. Frank says. "And these are my stepdaughters Ida, Isabelle, and Inez and my stepson, Ian." He could just as well say, "Hello, this is the wife and family I have stolen." Inez says it makes us more interesting. She wants to call Mr. Frank "Spapa" (short for step-papa) because people will notice and think she is mysterious. She has broken up with Charlie long-distance. How do you break up with a soldier? I was set on her marrying Charlie so he'd be my big brother. Her outlook has changed with college coming on in just three months. At least then I'll have my own room again.

Love from Your Daughter,
Isabelle

June 9, 1944

Dear Charlie,

Don't mind the letter you got from Inez. I know Inez pretty good, and I have seen how much she changes her mind. We are living on a new high-class street and the adjustment has gone to her head. She thinks she needs new friends to go along with the college life she is about to enter. Just keep writing to her so she doesn't forget you. I haven't forgotten the fun we all had with you around. She will remember, too.

Look out for those bullets!
Your friend,
Isabelle

June 10, 1944

Dear Aunt Izzy,

Now that the marriage is out in the open, we are going to meet Mr. Frank's family in St. Cloud. There is a mother and a father and four sisters and three brothers and more nieces and nephews than Mr. Frank can count. Aside from the sister that is a nun and the brother that is a priest, Mr. Frank is the last one to marry. I was going to offer to stay at Jordahls' while they were gone and teach Jimmy some letters and numbers, but then I might miss the nun. I have never seen one up close. I'm going to ask her if she has ears under the drape they wear on their heads. I did not see that on your list of things not to ask.

Love,
Isabelle

P. S. Mama moved her things from her room. Now she is all the way down two hallways and up the stairs. She put her clothes in the closet in Mr. Frank's room. There is only one bed. I looked in her drawers for her picture of Papa but couldn't find it, even in her underwear drawer.

June 10, 1944

Dear Eleanor,

Happy summer vacation! Remember the new house I told you about? Well, I need some help. Now I am going to be meeting some important people, like the ones that used to come to your house. Not a mayor, but a nun at least and who knows what all else in the future. I'm not so much worried about myself, but about my younger brother and sister. They have no showy talents like your piano playing to entertain people. Do you have to talk to the people or do you just go play and is there a kids' table for meals?

Let me know. Maybe I can visit you in Zumbrota this summer. I'll wait for an invitation, though.

From,
Isabelle

June 13, 1944

Dear Papa,

Don't go looking Mama up in the phone book. You won't find her on the Anderson page. I saw her sign her name today! It is Sophie Colletti!

"Well, my dear, that's how it's done when you get married," Mama told me. "Would you like it if we changed your name as well, and Ian and Ida's, too?" She smiled and stroked my hair but it felt like she hit me instead.

From,

Isabelle Anderson

June 16, 1944

Dear Papa,

In two days we are going to meet Mr. Frank's family in St. Cloud. It will be a picnic like we had in Zumbrota that time. I have a new sailor dress for the occasion. It matches Ida's and Inez's. Ian's clothes are matching too except they're boys'.

Mr. Frank's family will think he got himself a set of children out of the Sears catalog.

I have finished enough pages of the book about you that the fastener won't close. One chapter is all the jokes you told that I could remember. The mouse in the pumpkin one is still my favorite. I haven't even gotten to the "Death and Funeral" chapter. The book will have to have two volumes or longer fasteners. I am going to bring the book to St. Cloud. Eleanor says it is important to not talk too much among large groups of adults. She says it would be good to sit and read a book if one is tempted toward idle chatter. There may be a lot of children, too, but I will have my book in case no one wants to play with Stepchildren.

Mama has a nice dress for the outing, too. She sewed it herself. You would be very proud. "My lovely bride," you would say and twirl her around the kitchen. And she would say, "Heavens, Nils! The children!" and would pull away but she would have a smile on her face.

I'll write a report for you when we return.

Your daughter,

Isabelle

June 18, 1944

Dear Papa,

Happy Father's Day. Mama made us make cards for Mr. Frank today while he was at Mass (that's what they call a Catholic service). I wrote "Dear Sir, Thank you for the room and board. The paper, too. Sincerely, Isabelle Anderson."

Then I took an extra sheet and made a picture for you (enclosed). I made pictures of all the earth things you might be missing in heaven. Notice the cigar. I won't show Mama, just like I didn't used to tell.

I'd write more but have to show myself downstairs in this stiff dress. I must deliver my card, and then we are off to meet Them.

Love and hugs and kisses!

Isabelle

Dear Aunt Izzy,

They do have ears (nuns)! I'm not supposed to tell, but I will slip it just to you: Sister Carmelita plays cards! And once she swore (under her breath) and she burped in church. I can see why some people want to be Catholic if they have nuns like this one to talk to. But there are hard parts to nunning. They cannot eat except at the convent (that's the house where they all live together. Imagine. How do they tell each other apart? "Hey, you with the long dress, pass the bread." And they all reach for the bread. Ha-ha-ha-ha!) They cannot just leave the church whenever they want. Sister Carmelita had to get special "dispensation" (that's like permission when it comes from the Big Mother or someone like that at the house). And she had to bring another nun with her, even though she's just seeing her family. Sister Mary Margaret is very old. I don't think she does have ears under her scarf. She said "Amen" a lot. Sister Carmelita works at St. Joseph's Orphan Home on Randolph. She is much stricter there than at family gatherings, she said. That's where we were today. At Mr. Frank's family gathering.

If you would like to know more about all of this and me, please come out here and hear it in person. Mama's family doesn't come around because of the not approving of The Marriage, and you are all we have of Papa's family. If things go on like they did today, we will be swept clean into Mr. Frank's family and will not be Andersons at all.

Goodbye until I see you,
Isabelle Valborg Anderson

June 19, 1944

Dear Papa,
Here is an account of our trip to St. Cloud:
All of us kids were polite, even Ian.

Everyone was pleased to meet us, even the nun (even after I told her we are Lutheran. "You may want to keep that subject quiet today, child," she said).

The food was fine.

There are 40 nieces and nephews! Some are grown-up and the youngest one is two. I couldn't say how many were actually there because people moved around too much for me to get an accurate count. It was all civilians, though. I didn't see any uniforms. But they have 14 blue stars in the family and seven gold ones. That is two-thirds of their soldiers alive and one-third dead.

I did not get chummy with the other children, as they are not *cousins* like Mr. Frank says they are. Instead, I sat next to Mama at the meal, then with the nun afterward. I showed her the entire book about you. I'm sure she will pass word along to the rest of Mr. Frank's family that we already have a father, and his memory is papa enough for us. The nun (Sister Carmelita) kept the book for me when Mr. Frank asked me to help with croquet. I have unusual ability, he says.

One of the nieces said Mr. Frank is her favorite uncle. You must be very curious about this man who has taken your family. So I found that niece later and asked a few questions about him. He is fifty years old, which is ten years older than Mama is. He has always had a withered hand. She said the cousins used to call him "Uncle Born-That-Way" instead of "Uncle Frank," behind his back, of course. When he heard them once, they were scared he'd be mad. But instead he let them all measure their own long arms against his shorter one and shake his hand. He is a doctor but does not have patients. He is in charge of the hospital, which is why he has the big house. She (the niece) said that her grandparents are nearly as proud of Mr. Frank as they are of the son that is the priest. Her father is a mechanic but is off at the war so they are finally proud of him, too.

Some of the relatives tried to hug us when we left. When I saw them start in on Ida, I went to the bathroom. But I didn't stay long enough and three of them got me when I came out. I don't think they fully understand that they should not be so happy about this. If it were okay for Lutherans to marry Catholics and for a man like Mr. Frank to marry his cleaning lady with five children, then Uncle Bernard and Uncle Edgar would be inviting us all out, too. Maybe the nun filled them all in after we left.

From,

Isabelle Anderson

Dear Papa,

Today Mama said she was dishrag weary, which is funny because she hasn't been tired in a long time.

"How would you kids like to see a hospital?" Mr. Frank asked.

"No, thank you," I said. "I've been."

"You haven't been to this one," Mama said. In addition, Ian and Ida really wanted to go. Inez is helping out at the hospital all summer as a volunteer so she had no choice either and we all piled in the car and left Mama alone with the cleaning lady.

Mr. Frank knows everyone there. The doctors, the nurses, even some of the patients. He has a big office. He has a secretary named Janet outside his office who gave us juice.

Mr. Frank dragged us all over the building. Ida wanted to see the babies and Ian wanted to see blood. Mr. Frank had me recite the sea poem to several people we met along the way (the one you taught me: "I must go down to the sea again," and so on and so forth). He had Ian walk on his hands (right in the hallway!) and Ida pirouette. He clapped every time. He must not get much in the way of entertainment. Finally he took us home. Mama had finished a nap and made us lunch and we had to report all the details. I'll tell you this. I am not going to be a nurse when I grow up.

 Isabelle

June 23, 1944

Dear Papa,

 It's 95 degrees. Mama's wilting. I bring her cold water while she sits under the oak tree in the backyard. It is a big yard and lined with thick bushes so we can't see the neighbors. While Mama rests, I take Ian and Ida on adventures. The bushes are hollow in the middle. We crawl in and look at the neighbors' yards. We take a snack wrapped up in a hanky. We have explored the whole yard and at night Mama says she is proud of me for helping her keep things calm. I don't think she'll send me away again. I also make her cold cloths to put on her forehead and I read to her in the late afternoon, when it is the hottest. Mr. Frank frets over Mama. She lost a husband and a house and has all of us to be concerned with, I told him; she's bound to be tired.

Good night, Papa!

Isabelle Anderson

P. S. Here is my new prayer. I am going to teach it to Ida and Ian when Mama's not up to putting them to bed.

> *Now I lay me down to sleep.*
> *I pray the Lord my soul to keep.*
> *If I should die before I wake,*
> *Take me to Papa for heaven's sake.*

Dear Papa,

Someone moved into 1234 Palace! I heard Mr. Frank and Mama talking about it. I'm going there today to see for myself.

Isabelle

June 26, later

It is a family. Only a mother, though, just like us. The father was killed in the war and they all moved here from Chicago to be closer to their grandma and grandpa. They are Catholic and have a statue of the Blessed Virgin in the front garden. There are five kids just like us. But none of them as old as the twins. That mother has her basket full! I wonder if she gets as tired as Mama does.

Inez and Ian and Ida and me went there today while Mama rested. We pulled Ida in the wagon. First we went and picked up Jimmy. Mrs. Jordahl hugged us and fed us lunch even though we'd already eaten. We filled her in on everything happening on River Boulevard. I told her to be happy on Palace even though the houses are smaller here. Jimmy would not like River Boulevard. The sidewalks are so far down the lawn from the houses. She gave us a bunch of rhubarb from her garden to bring down to 1234. The mother was putting laundry on the line and two of the girls were hanging upside down by their knees from the laundry poles.

"Why didn't we ever try that when we lived here?" I said, and they jumped down and let us try. It brought my oatmeal to my throat and my dress to my waist so now I know. The kids were scared of Jimmy. We showed them how he can hopscotch. I said the main thing is not to laugh at him. Just pretend he is large for his age.

They said we could go in the house and look around but we didn't. There were boxes all over and none of the stuff coming out of them looked like our stuff. There's a gold star in the window for their father.

"Come over again," they said, and maybe we will.

Jimmy cried when we left Palace.

So there you go.

Isabelle Anderson

June 30, 1944

Dear Papa,

You will never guess who's here! Give up? Well, we were relaxing ourselves in the living room with the shades pulled this afternoon, as it is hot hot hot. Then comes the doorbell. "Who could that be?" says Mama, stretching her legs out in front of her, then curling them back up on her chair. The bell rings again. "Isabelle, would you get it?" I race through the hall to the front door. The lady standing there is just as tall as me. She's selling something I think because she has a big bag and looks all sweaty like she's been walking a ways. She doesn't look tidy like one of Mr. Frank's friends.

I look at her through the screen trying to think how Mama gets rid of people at the door.

When I'm going to give up thinking and just close the door, she says, "Isabelle, is that you?"

And of course it is me.

"Well, Miss Isabelle Valborg, I finally took your advice and here I am. Aren't you going to let your Aunt Izzy in?"

That's right, Papa! Your sister is here in this very house.

I jumped right out on that front step and hugged her hard. Once for you and once for me. I pulled her bag into the hall and it yowled! "Heavens, I forgot!" Aunt Izzy cried and unzipped the zipper and out leaped a skinny striped cat. It went streaking up the stairs and we haven't found it yet.

"Mama didn't tell me you were coming," I said.

"I didn't tell her," Aunt Izzy said.

"Man, oh man, oh man," I said, and we went to the living room.

"Isabelle?" Mama said.

"Yes?" Aunt Izzy and I said together. (Ha-ha-ha-ha.)

"Izzy, is that you?" Mama said. She stood up.

Papa, I wish I could tell you that Mama went over and gave Aunt Izzy a hug, too, but she didn't. After the "Well, I never!" she and A. I. started in on a whole list of who said and who did and so on. All about when you were in the hospital. It made my stomach hurt.

So, the tall and short of it is that Aunt Izzy is staying with us tonight. The grownups are downstairs talking now and I sat on the top step and tried to hear, but they were too quiet.

I am going to find that cat.

More when it happens,

Isabelle Anderson

P. S. She brought her ration stamps plus a whole bag of sugar! I'm almost for sure that we will have cake tomorrow!

P. P. S. She brought her roller skates, too! She must be over thirty years old and she roller-skates!

Dear Papa,

I am ten today. When you died, I was eight. I look pretty much the same except taller with bigger feet. I got lots of presents. Just like Eleanor. Roller skates, two dresses, paper, pencils, and from Aunt Izzy a picture frame. She put in it a picture she took of all of us when we were in California that one time. You had me on one knee and Ian on the other. Aunt Jaye sent me a box with embroidery supplies in it and a Luther's Small Catechism. "Remember you are Lutheran and we love you," she said in their card. Mr. Frank gave me a box. It is tin and has a picture of the Eiffel Tower in Paris on it. "For your special correspondence," he wrote. I don't know what he means, but I will put your letters in it. And he gave me Catholic beads called a rosary. They'd go nice with my sailor dress but are not to be worn as a necklace. He also gave me a storybook doll. Mine is a nun. Eleanor has the bride doll. Mama gave me a book. It has a green leather cover, soft as one of your car cloths. Inside are just lines, no words. "Write us some tall tales," Mama said. There was cake and ice cream. It was just the family, as too many people wear Mama out, but that was okay. Uncle Bernard, Aunt Jaye, and the rest are probably busy planning their Fourth of July party anyhow.

Your double-digit daughter,
Isabelle Anderson

July 3, 1944

Dear Papa,

Aunt Izzy is still here. She can't buy 1234 of course, which I had planned. She is only here for a visit after all. Mama let her stay here even though she did not come for your funeral. Mr. Frank likes Aunt Izzy. The cat (Mr. Right) likes Ian. Aunt Izzy played with us kids while Mama rested. Aunt Izzy can raise one eyebrow up at a time, just like you did. She has a high voice like a lonely bird. I guess you know all that. But maybe you don't know this. She moved to California for LOVE! It didn't work out though. He did not go to church or believe in God. She thought Love was bigger than God. But she found out it isn't and she ended up with a cat instead.

Tomorrow is Independence Day. I wonder what they are doing in Zumbrota.

Love,

Isabelle Anderson

July 4, 1944

Dear Papa,

Did you see the fireworks in heaven? We stayed up until dark and Mr. Frank lit sparklers in the backyard. We were going to go to his family picnic today but Mama didn't feel good.

Happy Birthday to the United States of America.

Love,

Isabelle Anderson

July 5, 1944

Dear Papa,

Guess who is going to have a baby?!
From,
Isabelle Anderson

July 6, 1944

Dear Papa,

Will Mama still want us here when Mr. Frank is the papa of this baby?
From,
Isabelle Anderson

July 7, 1944

Dear Papa,

Will the new baby be Catholic or Lutheran? When we all die, will the baby go to heaven like us? Aunt Izzy doesn't seem to know for sure.
Still hot,
Isabelle Anderson

Dear Papa,

The baby will come at Christmastime. That's a long time for Mama to be tired. She's tired, Papa, but this time her spirits are high.

Aunt Izzy is helping me with the book about you. She said there were quite a few things that weren't exactly right but that I could leave it as it is and just call it Historical Fiction. That sounds like it should go in a library so I am going to continue. We are adding a chapter about the shenanigans you pulled as a boy. I am letting her write that one. I asked Mama if I could interview her for the "Courting, Marriage, and Early Years of Family Life" chapter but she said that book's been written, read, and put on the shelf. I'll have to look for it. Ian is getting to be a good artist like Jimmy so I asked him to make lots of drawings. I am even letting him use some of the new pencils that came with my birthday pack of paper. I hope we see the nun again so I can show her the completed book.

From,

Who else?

July 13, 1944

Dear Papa,

The train took Aunt Izzy away today. It was all packed with servicemen going to meet Uncle Sam. They were hanging out of the windows in their sailor hats. Their duffel bags were crowding the floor. There almost wasn't room for her.

I had just gotten used to having Aunt Izzy comb my hair and stir up the talk at dinner and now she's gone. Who will play cribbage with me? She left her board here. She was going to leave Mr. Right, too, but when she heard our history with pets she decided to let us visit him instead. Mama and Aunt Izzy hugged and hugged today. Mama cried. I want to tie a string on the wrists of all my favorite people and tie them all to my wrist. Going to the bathroom would be a problem.

The baby will be Mr. Frank's real child and Mama's real child but my half brother or sister. Will the baby be related to you at all? I should have asked Aunt Izzy before she left.

With love,
Isabelle V. Anderson

Dear Papa,

    Seven weeks until school starts.

    "Why don't you get out and play with some neighborhood children?" Mama asks.

    I believe I will.

    On my way out,
    Isabelle

July 15, 1944

Dear Papa,

    I led Ian and Ida on an adventure today to stay out of Mama's way. We walked twice all the way around the block and drew a map of where the houses are and which ones we think have children. Then we picked out one where the children were outside and walked on up.

    We met Sylvia, Betty, and Shirley — named after Shirley Temple — ten, eight, and six. Their house looks all-covered-in-vines spooky and they said it is spooky inside, too, except they are used to it. Probably ghosts live on the third floor, Betty said.

"Ha!" said Ian.

"We'll show you," said Shirley, and they did. We didn't see any ghosts and didn't hear any either but we pretended we were hiding out from Nazis. Ian was the air raid warden. Then we played we were orphans. They had never met any stepchildren before or anyone whose father died of an allergic reaction or ran a filling station. They go to private school.

We're going back to their house tomorrow.

From,

Isabelle

July 20, 1944

Dear Eleanor,

Hi! How are you? I am fine. I have some new friends. You would like them, too. They live in a haunted house. I am going to get another brother or sister. Do you see my Aunt Jaye and Uncle Bernard? Do you play with Sue Joan Warick or any of the other kids from school? What about LeRoy Pence? Are there any more stars in the windows on Grandview?

From,
Isabelle

Dear Aunt Izzy,

We found one of Mr. Right's cat toys under Ian's bed. We will save it here for your next visit, which I hope will be soon. How much does it cost to ride the train? Maybe I could come and visit you in California. I will wait for an invitation, though. I am sure it would be educational to visit another state. I could help you plant a victory garden. We are working hard on ours. The corn is up to my waist almost. The visit will have to be after July, though, because we are pretty busy playing with the girls at the corner house, the one with all the vines. We are turning their third floor into our clubhouse. The Chatty Pigtails is the name of our club. Ian doesn't have a pigtail but he can join anyhow. If you would like to send us a postcard, we will put it on the clubhouse wall. Mama is going to write a note to you on the back of my letter. Bye!

Isabelle

July 23, 1944

Dear Irma,

Have you forgotten us? Mama is going to have a baby. Inez is signed up for college at St. Catherine's. It is okay, she says, because Mr. Frank (who's really Dr. Frank) is Catholic. Are you going to go to college? I am not so much of a cry-baby as you remember from before we moved. Ida is, though. Ian is as tall as me and has bigger feet. How about you?

Your sister (but not in the nun way!),

Isabelle

Dear Papa,

Mr. Frank smokes a pipe. It is his birthday so we gave him a new pipe. Mama gave us the money and we took the streetcar downtown like the old days. She told us right where to find one and we did. He is really Dr. Frank. But I am used to Mr. Frank by now.

From,

Isabelle

August 13, 1944

Dear Papa,

Mama is getting a big belly under her dress. Big enough that people at church know she has a baby under there. We haven't been to church in a long time, but we went back this week.

"Hold your head high, smile, and don't give out unnecessary details," Mama told us on the way there. She walked us clear up to the fourth row, where everyone could stare at the back of our heads. I liked it when you used to lead us into the back pew. "Easy in, easy out," you said, and you were right. From the front rows it is not easy out. We had to creep up the aisle afterward, talking to every busymind. I held my head so high my neck hurts. My face hurts from smiling. Mama shared the basics of her story with all the ladies. Remarried, enjoying life on Mississippi River Boulevard, looking forward to the little Christmas present. Just enough there to keep Beverly's mother filling in the details for weeks. I hope we don't do that again soon! What will happen if we keep not going to church, though?

From,

Isabelle

Dear Papa,

I think Mama doesn't want to go back to church anymore. I heard her ask Mr. Frank what it would take to get us all changed to Catholic.

So today I started Lutheran lessons for Ian and Ida. I heard about purgatory from Eleanor and I don't want us floating around space for years waiting to see you. I brought the Luther's Small Catechism from Aunt Jaye to our clubhouse at Sylvia, Betty, and Shirley's. They don't have one Bible in the house so I brought over one of ours. No one will miss it, as it was very dusty on the top shelf. They don't go to any church at all so they are in on the lessons, too.

Maybe Mr. Frank is the wolf in sheep's clothing that Pastor Grindahl was talking about in last Sunday's sermon. Maybe the Catholics sent him to get another family for their church. I gave him back the rosary beads and reminded him that we are Lutheran.

Don't worry. We will be ready to stand up for Lutherans.

Today's lesson was the Ten Commandments.

Honoring my father,

Isabelle

August 21, 1944

Dear Papa,

Sylvia, Betty, and Shirley are gone clear until school starts. We forgot they were leaving today and left all our things in the clubhouse. Now we have no catechism to study and Ian's baseball card collection is there, too. If we borrow a Bible and a hymnal and a catechism from the church, would that be stealing? We would be saving members for the church. I'd ask Pastor Grindahl but I don't want to have to share any unnecessary details.

From,

Isabelle

Dear Papa,

Mr. Frank is taking us all to a lake cottage for a week. He has traded meat stamps for gas stamps with one of the people at the hospital. He thinks the cool lake breezes would be good for Mama. We have no choice, of course. If we stay here, we have lots of gas but no meat. But look at the date of my letter. If we go now we will miss the State Fair! NO FAIR! I think he really is a spy sent from the Catholics. I'll bet we have to catch fish on Friday, too.

Notice that we will be out of town for two Sundays. That will bring our total of church services missed to 11 this summer, with only one attended. That is one thing Mr. Frank and Mama argue about. He goes to Mass on first Fridays and on Sundays and to Novena on Wednesdays. He says he prays for us. I hope God doesn't count those Catholic prayers against us. Probably Aunt Jaye's prayers cancel his out.

It doesn't bother me so much as I thought it would, not going to church on a Sunday morning, or missing Sunday school either. Actually Sunday mornings have been rather relaxing. Ida and Ian come on in my room where I lead them in a little service, just to let Jesus know we are not heathens or Catholics. Then we pretty much get to do as we please as long as we keep it down.

From,

Isabelle

August 24, 1944

Dear Eleanor,

I am sorry I will not be able to invite you to go to the State Fair this year. My family is going on Vacation. We will be driving north for more than three hours to stay at a Lake Resort.

Maybe next summer.

From,

Isabelle

Dear Papa,

Rabbit Lake has no rabbits that I can see, but there is a lake for sure. There are six cabins here and six docks. We have one of each plus a rowboat. All the kids sleep in one room. Kind of like the old days on Palace with me and Ida together again. The sun shines only on the lake because the pines are so thick on land. I am sitting in one right now! Seven branches up from the ground. It smells like Christmas in here.

This is a picture of Ian dropping an oar in the middle of Rabbit Lake. The other boat is Mr. Finley from the next cabin over rowing to our rescue.

Your camper,
Isabelle

Dear Aunt Izzy,

Hello from the North! We are at Rabbit Lake Resort. Ian has poison ivy on his legs. Mr. Right would love it here. There are mice in all the cabins. You would like it, too. There is lots of time for games. I have been playing whist with some kids at the lodge. Being Catholic still applies on vacation, but fish does taste better when you catch it yourself. Maybe next year you could come with us!

Love,
Isabelle

August 29, 1944

Dear Papa,

Hello again from Rabbit Lake!

I've been thinking about what I have told you so far about Mr. Frank. Maybe I have given you a bad impression. Since he never knew you, he couldn't have meant to actually steal your family. I am looking out for the Lutheran Church, though.

I learned to fish! I caught four yesterday, a new family record. Maybe they'll put my big one on the wall next to the deer head in the lodge.

Love from your girl,

Isabelle

August 30, 1944

Dear Papa,

Mama and I sat under the willow today while the rest of them fished. Turns out Mama was joking with Mr. Frank about turning Catholic.

"You have to laugh or you'll fall apart," Mama says. And listening in on conversations is eavesdropping. Even if it was done from the stairs and not from the eaves it will get you in trouble every time, she says. But this is the first time it has gotten me in trouble. More often it is very informational.

Mama thinks I will have the most talent to help with the baby. I was hoping for talent to play the piano, but everyone has to start somewhere. At least she'll need me around.

Love,
Isabelle

Dear Papa,

We have to leave Rabbit Lake tomorrow. I am polka-dotted with mosquito bites. I have picked wild mint. I have caught 12 or more fish since my last letter. I will miss eating meals at long tables in the lodge.

Did you know that Mr. Frank's father died when he was eight? Just like me. His mother got married again and that is the father I met in St. Cloud. I did not even know that Mr. Frank was a stepchild himself. You'd never know it to look at him.

Love to you from me,
Isabelle

September 2, 1944

Dear Papa,

We are back home. On the drive to St. Paul, we gave ideas for naming the baby. Mama and Mr. Frank said we could choose the name!

I put Nils on the boy's list but Ian's name is really Nils and his middle name is Ian. Of course you know that but why didn't I? We should call him Nils if that is his name. Mama said the baby doesn't have to have an "I" name like the rest of us. Good thing. How many other good "I" names are there? Ichabod, Ivy (I like that one), Irwin . . . It will be easier to branch out. It does have to be a saint's name, though. Where do you find those?

Was your favorite color blue or red?

Isabelle

September 5, 1944

Dear Papa,

Today was the first day of fifth grade. My teacher is Miss Green. We had to write a paragraph to introduce ourselves. I watched her eyes when she read I was a stepdaughter but she didn't so much as blink.

"Is your dad Dr. Colletti?" she said.

Well, I didn't know what to say.

"He was a classmate of my brother's," she said and went right on to James's desk.

No one must have remembered our fights from last year because I found three girls to eat with at lunch.

On to homework.

Isabelle

P. S. What do they feed you in heaven? Do you have to cook? I hope not. Heaven just wouldn't be eternal bliss with toast for every meal. (Not that your toast was bad, of course.)

Dear Papa,

Happy Birthday to You! It was handy for you to be born in the first year of the century because I will always know your age. Just think, if you'd lived to be 100, you would have been 100 in 2000!

I knew right when I woke up today that it was your birthday. I looked at everyone's face at breakfast to see if they remembered. Mama was rubbing her forehead and her belly. Ian was picking a scab and Ida was counting everything square in the kitchen trying to get to 50. Mr. Frank was already at work.

"September 19 and sunny!" I said, just to open the subject.

Mama looked cross at me and asked Ian if he'd finished his homework.

"September 19 is a big day in this family," I said.

"What!" Ida squealed. "Is it my birthday?"

"No, it is your Papa's birthday," I told her.

"But we just got him a pipe in the summer," Ida said.

"She means your *other* Papa," Ian said. "The one who's gone."

"That's enough, Isabelle," Mama said. "We all loved your father very much. But we are not going to celebrate his birthdays anymore. We don't want to hurt Papa Frank's feelings, now do we?"

On the way to school, I invited Ian to come to my room for a party after school. We snuck up some crackers and milk and taped paper candles to the crackers. (Only six, though, not the full 44.) We told 44 things we remember about you.

"Papa's laugh didn't have any sound. His mouth opened wide wide and his shoulders shook," I said.

"Papa was a good drawer. He could draw every kind of car," said Ian. "Papa yelled loud when he was mad."

"Papa didn't get mad very much," I said.

There are 40 more, but now my hand is tired.

Love,

Isabelle

Dear Aunt Izzy,

None of the Chatty Pigtails go to church. Sylvia says it is what we feel in our hearts that counts. Her dad says enjoying nature is getting as close to God as he needs. If I wanted to go to the Lutheran Church, I'd have to go alone now. Mama goes to Mass sometimes with Mr. Frank, and once she took the two little kids, but usually he goes alone and we stay home. Mama feels no more need for organized religion. What do you think?

I am writing a report about Minnesota for school. It takes a lot of my time. If the penmanship isn't perfect, Miss Green will return it, she says.

Love,
Isabelle

Dear Papa,

I have a new best friend. Her name is Mary and we both like peas but not beets. We are the exact same height and neither of us has a father. (Hers died in the war, of course.) Roller skating is our favorite sport. We are going to skate every day until it snows. Mary lives three blocks closer to school than we do so I pick her up on the way. She sings where I do not, but we are both Lutheran. She is in the choir at Our Savior's and has invited me to join her. Thanks all the same, I told her, but I am not currently attending services. She said I could just come to practice. Maybe I will.

Bye!

Isabelle

Dear Papa,

Irma has had word from Stuart. He is still alive. No one has heard from Charlie, though. If there really is such a thing as guardian angels, could you send one out to look for him?

Mama's baby is going to be big, judging from the size of her dresses. There are more Responsibilities around here for everyone now.

From,
Isabelle

December 18, 1944

Dear Papa,

Christmas vacation at last! Mary and I plan to ice-skate every day with the Chatty Pigtails.

Everyone is watching Mama now. When she coughs, Mr. Frank jumps. When she sighs, we all put our forks down.

"I've done this before, everyone," Mama says. "Watching me won't make it happen any quicker."

We try to act like we aren't watching, but we are. I'll let you know as soon as it's born!

Love,

Isabelle

December 25, 1944

Dear Papa,

Ian got a brother! (The rest of us, too.) Franklin Delano Colletti was born today along with Jesus. (Did you know that there is a town in Minnesota named Delano?) Mama is fine and Mr. Frank says we can all go to the hospital tomorrow to see them both. Ida moved into my room and we made her room all over for Franklin. We'll call him Frankie, I think. (Or we could call him Mr. President!)

I embroidered a towel for him to be a baby blanket. I'm going to wrap him all up and rock him back and forth and tell him stories of his step-papa Nils.

Merry Christmas!

Love,

Isabelle

⟸1945⟹

January 6, 1945

Dear Aunt Izzy,

Thank you for the Christmas presents for all of us. Frankie will love his teddy bear. For now, Ida is sleeping with it. I love the blouse you sewed me but I will have to wait a while to wear it. We wear long sleeves in Minnesota nearly until June, at least until May.

This is a drawing of little Frankie. He is about as light to hold as a slice of toast. Well, maybe a whole sandwich, but light.

Love,
Isabelle

January 18, 1945

Dear Papa,

I am finding that I do not have such a talent for babies. Frankie cries when I hold him and I stuck him with a diaper pin twice. He makes me impatient with all his sleeping. Ian hopes he grows up fast. Mama says we cried in the night, too. Is that true? Frankie does not look much like the rest of us. His hair is black. His eyes are brown.

More soon,
Isabelle

P. S. I'm wondering if Frankie is Catholic. Isn't it about time for a baptism?

February 12, 1945

Dear Papa,

Mama does not want me calling Mr. Frank "Mr. Frank" anymore. She says it embarrasses her in public. She says it hurts Mr. Frank's feelings because Ida and Ian call him "Papa Frank" and sometimes just plain "Papa." I've heard them. She thinks it is high time I do that, too.

"I can't change history," I told her. She sent me to my room for the duration of the evening. Don't worry, I'll stick by you no matter what.

For the duration. For the duration — everyone says that about the war. I think it must be heaven to be in peace and not lick one war stamp or savings stamp into a book ever again.

Your girl,

Isabelle

February 26, 1945

Dear Papa,

Frankie is Catholic! We went to Mass! In the Catholic Church!

Mama signed a paper when the priest blessed them that said all the children they have together would be Catholic. That showed no foresight, which she is always saying I need to have.

The Mass was for Frankie's baptism. All Mr. Frank's family was there from the picnic last summer. We were the only ones from our family there. They had to call Frankie "Francis" just for the baptism because all Catholics have to have a saint's name and "Franklin" isn't a saint. "What about the president?" I asked. "He's Franklin."

"He's not Catholic, and besides, there's more to it," Mr. Frank said. "For one thing, you have to be dead to be a saint." I hope there is no Saint Isabelle so I don't have to worry about the Catholics wanting me for their church.

I do kind of like Frankie even with the crying and messes. I feel bad that I won't see him in heaven. Irma told me so. At least he'll have Mr. Frank.

From the Lutheran side of the house,
Isabelle

P. S. I can see why the Catholics like to go to church, though. They have lots of little candles that anyone can light and ceilings nearly to heaven and colored windows. Those women who decorate our church should peek in for ideas.

March 5, 1945

Dear Aunt Izzy,

This is a holy card. Remember the sister I told you about with the ears? Well, I saw her again, and the rest of Mr. Frank's family, because Frankie got baptized. Sister Carmelita gave me a stack of these cards. They are all about saints and I have read them, every one. I don't think I should throw them away but it can't be right for me to keep them. Would you please write me what you think I should do? My friend Mary says to keep them would be a sin but to give them back would be impolite. I could take them over to the orphan home or use them in an art project or bring them to Jimmy. Or should I give them back?

Catholics (except Jordahls) seem to have a whole pile of kids in every family. Do you think that Mama will have more babies now that half of her marriage is Catholic?

Wondering and waiting to hear from you,
Isabelle

March 19, 1945

Dear Papa,

Mama won't give up on the "Papa Frank" thing. Was she this stubborn when you knew her? Mr. Frank has not said anything to me about it.

But to do my part for peace, I have found a solution. I will now call Mr. Frank nothing. I won't call him "Nothing." I just won't say anything. There really is no reason to say a name for him at all. "Please pass the butter" (if it weren't so rationed) works the same as "Please pass the butter, Papa." No one will notice, even.

Love,
Isabelle

March 22, 1945

Dear Papa,

Three days and my plan is still working! I have not called Mr. Frank anything. I had a close call tonight when I needed to ask him a question and he was reading the paper. I coughed loud, which until this time has worked (he's a doctor, you'll remember). I went and stood by the fireplace in front of him. Nothing. I straightened the picture on the mantel rather loudly. Still he held the paper in front of his face. Finally, I walked past the side of his chair and accidentally bumped him. He had fallen asleep reading the paper! He woke up with a jolt and said, "What's the matter? What's the matter!" By then I'd forgotten what I was going to ask so I told him Mother needed him and went upstairs and here I am.

From,

Isabelle

April 10, 1945

Dear Papa,

Do you hear everything we say? If so, were you listening today just before dinner? If so, I didn't mean to hurt your feelings. I was so mad about what happened at school today and Mama was busy with Frankie, and Ida and Ian were fighting and then Mr. Frank came home and chose me out of the whole crowd of us to lean his shorter arm on and ask "How's things?" and then I spilled it all out and told him about getting four wrong on the spelling test and my teacher announcing the scores out loud and the puddle on the way home and I even called him *Papa* Frank. I didn't mean to. If I were Catholic, I could go to confession. But I pulled it together by dinner and just told my lost sheep joke and came up here to do my homework.

Good night,
Isabelle

April 12, 1945

Dear Papa,

First you, then LeRoy Pence's father, then lots more people's fathers and uncles and brothers and cousins.

And today, President Franklin Delano Roosevelt died. Have you met him yet? If so, tell him that everyone here is sad. His voice has been coming through the radio as long as I've been listening. He's been my only president. What will happen now?

In memory of The President,
Isabelle

April 15, 1945

Dear Papa,

Even before President Roosevelt's funeral there is a new president. Mr. Harry S. Truman. I hope he knows what he's doing.

Yours,
Isabelle

April 25, 1945

Dear Papa,

I am in my room until further notice. Disrespect is the charge. I called Mr. Frank "Frank." How is that disrespectful? It is not like he is a stranger or someone at church or something. Mama was talking at me all the way up the stairs. It was a comedown-when-you-have-a-better-attitude speech. Remember those? It used to be mostly Irma who got them. Now I know how she felt. Maybe if I'd called him "Francis" instead. At least with you it was easy. Except that one time I called you Pops.

I.V.A.

May 6, 1945

Dear Aunt Izzy,

Thank you for the postcard. Did you hear about President R? At least Mrs. Roosevelt has their dog, Fala.

I still have half of the holy cards. I shared them with my friend Mary. They are under my bed. I suppose you're right. It hasn't harmed me so far to keep them. They would be nice to collect, if I weren't Lutheran. Don't we have any beads or cards or statues or anything to pass around?

Your niece,

Isabelle

June 2, 1945

Dear Papa,

I am wondering about something. I wish I could see your face because I don't know what you will feel about this. You are my Papa and will always be my true father. It is just confusing at school and in conversation about Mr. Frank. What if I just called him "Dad"? I looked it up in my dictionary and one meaning is "father" but the other one is "fellow, buddy, pal (usually in addressing a stranger)." So you see, Mr. Frank is not a stranger even, and people know the term and everything. Some people call their fathers "Dad" but we called our father "Papa." So "Dad" is different. I will think about it some more, but I wanted to try it out on you first.

Wondering,
Isabelle

June 8, 1945

Dear Papa,

I have thought about the "Dad" thing and didn't get any bad feelings from thinking about it. So I had a talk with Mr. Frank tonight. He thought it would be fine if I called him "Dad." He got weepy and tried to hug me with his long arm and said he loved me.

I wish I could tell what you think.
Still Your Girl,
Isabelle

August 14, 1945

Dear Papa,

VICTORY! The war is over over over! Can you hear the shouts up there? Everyone is dancing in the street. I'm going out there, too! Thought you'd want to know! Tell Mr. Roosevelt!

Do you remember peace days? I wish you could tell me what to expect.

I guess I could ask Dad. As long as you aren't right here.

Hurrah for America!
Isabelle

September 19, 1945

Dear Papa,

Happy Birthday! Mary and I sang to you on the way home from school today. Did you hear us? Then we sang "My Country, 'Tis of Thee" and "You're a Grand Old Flag." Mary wants to make a Joy Singer out of me (that's her choir).

Hope there's cake in heaven!
Love,
Isabelle

P. S. The war is still over.

October 3, 1945

GUESS WHAT, PAPA!

Stuart is back — in one piece! Irma hadn't heard from him since the war ended and no one knew when he'd come home. Here is what happened and I am not kidding: Irma was here for a visit hoping to get news when Stuart's parents heard. She and I went downtown on the streetcar to pass the afternoon. We dilly-dallied around, saw a show, and got back on the streetcar.

"IRMA?" we heard from the back of the car and turned around. THERE WAS STUART in his uniform! She screamed and pushed through the crowd to the back and they hugged and KISSED and everyone clapped. The old lady next to me honked her nose in a hanky. Irma stayed on the streetcar all the way to Stuart's house but I had to get off at St. Clair. I'm going to ask Stuart about Charlie the next time I see him.

Hurrah!

Isabelle

November 16, 1945

Dear Aunt Izzy,

I am having a friend problem. You see, Mary is my best friend. But Sylvia from the Chatty Pigtails is my friend, too. Mary and I always skate after school or at least sit on her step and talk. And on Fridays I usually stay and eat dinner at her house. We don't plan it; it just works out that way. Well, Sylvia invited me to go to the new Jimmy Stewart movie with her this Friday. Her mother said she could invite one friend and go to a show because her sisters are going to a birthday party. I said yes right away, but then when I told Mary, she was hurt and mad. We had plans, she said.

It was easier when I didn't have a best friend.

By the way, Ida got caught wearing rosary beads to school as a necklace. Dad was actually angry with her. Then he and Mama argued about church and you'd think the war had started again. Ida shut herself in the closet. Frankie cried and I had to read to him. Don't you want to come back for a visit?

Your niece,
Isabelle

December 20, 1945

Dear Aunt Izzy,

I'm glad you had friend trouble, too. Well, not glad that you did, but glad that you understand. Mary didn't wait for me after school for about two weeks. Sylvia has friends from St. Paul Academy that are funny and wild. I was so happy that she still wanted to be my friend that I did go with her, but this weekend all three of us are going to go to a show.

Thanks for the knitting patterns. I'm sure they will come in handy someday.

Merry Christmas and Happy Birthday (almost) to Franklin!

Love,

Isabelle

❖1946❖

March 17, 1946

Dear Papa,

About peace (you must be wondering, since it's been here seven months): The uniforms are gone and it's funny to see men wearing suits and ties. Sister Carmelita says since there is no fabric ration, women's skirts should be long enough to cover their knees. But they aren't. Most of the rationing is over. Your station is busy, I'll bet. We ate steak for an end-of-ration celebration. And we all got new shoes, even Frankie, who runs everywhere now. Most of all, though, Charlie didn't come back. Blown to bits in Burma. I hope you have gotten to meet him in heaven. I miss him.

Love,

Isabelle

Dear Papa,

Mary is moving away! We have been through two grades together. She is moving to Fargo, North Dakota. The wind blows people off the sidewalks there, she says. She doesn't want to go. We are praying that her mother finds a doctor to marry so she can live on Mississippi River Boulevard and not have to go to work. Stuart says the women are supposed to give jobs back to the men anyhow.

Do you have any pull in this department?

Your almost-twelve-year-old,

Isabelle

August 30, 1946

Dear Papa,

I have lots of friends now. Not like earlier. This summer I have gotten back in with Sylvia's crowd. I don't get influenced so how can they be bad influences?

"We don't like who you are becoming,"

Mama and Dad say. They talk about sending me to Catholic school. What? Catholics don't smoke an occasional cigarette? Maybe they just don't get caught. I will NOT be converted!

Feeling irascible (adj., easily provoked to anger),

Isabelle

September 15, 1946

Dear Papa,

I am still in public school. I had to promise to study, come right home after school, and help with more chores around the house. School and after school are not the same without Mary. Sylvia and her group went right on having fun without me. I've seen them going into her house.

Ian is the chess champion of the whole school and Ida plays the violin. Plus she sings. "Voice of an angel," Dad says. Have you heard her? What do *I* do?

Yours truly,

Isabelle

← 1947–1950 →

March 12, 1947

Dear Papa,

Mama is upset because she ran into my math teacher at Nile Drug. "Isabelle is not applying herself," she said. "She is more focused on her social relationships than her schoolwork." SO? I am not a procrastinator as Mother says. I just lack interest in the pursuits which have been put before me up to this date. If you were here, you wouldn't be this upset. After all, you did not go to college. You could make her understand that education is not the Living End. Dad just nods at me when Mama is giving her sermons. Now I have to do just enough so they don't put me in parochial school.

Yours,

Isabelle

May 3, 1947

Dear Papa,

I've had it with classes like Home Economics and Physical Education. I want to EXPLORE. See the WORLD. This town is keeping me down. Why hasn't Dad thought of travel for this family? He has the money. James Horner's family travels all the time. He has even been to Canada.

Unhappily yours,
Isabelle

P. S. You would have taken me places, wouldn't you?

July 14, 1947

Dear Papa,

I look lovely today. I have a new organdy dress. What is the occasion, you may wonder? A WEDDING! Irma and Stuart are married! Inez and I stood up with her and Ida was a flower girl. Irma looked as near to one of your angel friends as we'll ever see here on Earth. I hope someday I have a wedding like this one along with a cute new house like the one Irma and Stuart are moving into over in Falcon Heights.

Uncle Edgar came to walk her down the aisle. Mr. Frank would have been honored to stand in for you, only he cannot go to a Lutheran Church service. He came to the reception even though it was in the church basement. I promised not to mention it to Sister Carmelita.

Uncle Bernard and Aunt Jaye were there. They sat on the groom's side in the back and didn't stay for the reception, but I saw them when I walked down the aisle and I know Irma did, too. At least they came.

Does having a married daughter make you feel old? It does Mama.

Love and hugs,

Isabelle

November 30, 1947

Dear Papa or should I say GRANDFATHER!

Irma is going to have a baby! She doesn't look like it yet but it is for real, she said. I have promised to baby-sit. The baby will come in May. I'll be an aunt. I'll let you know as soon as it is born.

XOXOXO,
Isabelle

January 9, 1948

Dear Aunt Izzy,

Thank you for the baby yarn and patterns. I still have not learned to knit, but Mama said she would teach me so I can make things for the baby. Maybe after that I will make myself a red hat. I would like to see a picture of Mr. Right in the sweater you made him for Christmas!

Love,
Isabelle

May 23, 1948

Dear Papa,

I am an AUNT! Eunice Marie Swanson has arrived. We get to go see her on Wednesday. Wish you could come see her, too. Her nickname will be Eunie.

Love,
Isabelle

September 21, 1948

Dear Papa,

Here I am. Still in St. Paul. The farthest we got this summer was Rabbit Lake. Like every summer.

However, I can earn my own money and then I'll travel. I am going to go over to the drugstore after school tomorrow and ask about a job. My first trip will be to California to see Aunt Izzy. I've been so bad about writing to her but I am sure she will let me come out anyhow.

How do you like them apples?

Love,

Isabelle

P. S. A late Happy Birthday!

September 22, 1948

Dear Papa,

Bad idea! I got home late today on account of walking to the drugstore after school. Mama was m-a-d mad. She'd already called Dad to go drive around looking for me.

When they found out what I was "up to" (even though the drugstore does not need help at the present time), they said, "Jobs at the drugstore are for girls from families who need the money. If you need something to keep you busy, we'll find something to keep you busy."

That wasn't the point, but again, they just don't understand. So Dad jumped right to the phone, called Sister Carmelita, and has lined up for me to go work for the sisters at St. Joseph's Orphan Home! Like I said before, I don't have a talent for babies, and that goes for older children, too. But it is settled. I will start next week.

I.V.A.

November 11, 1948

Dear Papa,

We are back in the fold. Mama has decided that we should return to church so I can be con-firmed.

"I already started drinking coffee," I told her, "so what's the point?"

"Don't get smart with me," she said.

"I thought you wanted me to be smart," I said. And now I have to go to confirmation classes and stay in my room after school for a week. Is your mother in heaven? (I'm sure she is.) I'll bet it is much easier to get along with her there.

I.V.A.

November 12, 1948

Dear Papa,

Punishing me with a week in my room is really punishing the orphans. I will miss two afternoons at St. Joseph's. Those children depend on me. One boy, who is about the age Ian was when you died, will only speak out loud to me. To everyone else he just shakes or nods his head, depending on the situation. He saves up all kinds of stories for me, and I tell the whole group of orphans some of mine. I have had to start planning ahead though, as Sister Carmelita wants to know in advance what my story topic will be. She did not approve of last month's story, though the children liked it very much. The sisters don't get out to movies so they don't understand modern society. These poor orphans are going to be mighty surprised when they leave here and find the rest of the world out there. For one thing, they all wear light blue uniforms every day. Choosing a wardrobe alone will be a daunting (adj., discouraging) task. I try to wear something up-to-date when I go so they can get some ideas.

I have a long evening ahead. I will draw you some pictures of current styles and of some movie stars, too.

Love,

Izzy (My friends call me that now! It makes Mother roll her eyes.)

March 11, 1949

Dear Papa,

Confirmation classes have not answered my question. How exactly are Catholics and Lutherans different to God? We only had a few lessons on Martin Luther, which started to explain things, but when the hour is up, there is no more time for questions.

It is strange to be Lutheran and go home from confirmation class and see Dad starving himself to get a soul out of purgatory, something Catholics do during Lent. I asked Pastor Grindahl if Lutherans could get sent to purgatory, but he just said, "Let's stick to the text, please."

Not much other news.

I don't write often, but your picture is still on my wall.

Love,

Izzy

October 20, 1949

Dear Papa,

I did get confirmed after all. It was a bit close, as I didn't pass the interview the first time. I still can't believe they REALLY mean that the wine turns into Jesus' blood at communion. I can't think of it that way or I gag up there at the altar, but I finally said I believed it because Mama had a big party planned and there wasn't time to call it off.

All our family was at the party. Aunt Jaye and Uncle Bernard came and Uncle Edgar, too. Dad couldn't come to the service but he bought a corsage for my dress. I've decided something, Papa, and I hope with your experience up there you'll agree with me. From what I can tell, Catholics and Lutherans have the same God. It has been a lot of work keeping our holy cards and

Luther's Small Catechism and everything else separate. I don't think God would mind if our whole family went to a church service together sometimes, even if it is the Catholic service. I guess he'd just as soon hear me singing Catholic hymns as no hymns, and we say the Lord's Prayer both places. I know by now you can't tell me what you think, but there it is.

Mama always said we could start drinking coffee when we were confirmed but I have been doing it for years. So I don't feel too different.

XOXOXO,

Izzy

May 9, 1950

Dear Papa,

Edward Johnson threw a little stone up at my window this evening. Ed is so tall he has to stoop to get through the doors at school. He can whistle any tune you can name and his smile is absolutely dreamy. Dad saw him out there and invited him in.

"Come on in, young man," Dad said. "Better to talk to her than break her window."

Thank goodness Ed had the presence of mind to say he must have the wrong house. He escaped through the backyard.

You would like him.

Love,

Izzy

May 13, 1950

Dear Papa,

Turns out Ed had the wrong window after all. He and Sylvia on the corner are now going steady. My heart has been torn asunder.

Your girl,

Izzy

❖1957❖

Dear Papa,

I haven't written now in seven years, but that doesn't mean I don't think about you. It's Christmas and I'm home with Mama and the whole family. One of my packages this year held the tin box with the Paris picture on it from my tenth birthday. It is filled with a stack of letters written in the wide cursive handwriting of a young girl. Our letters, Papa. It's been so long, I'd nearly forgotten them.

A lot has changed on Mississippi River Boulevard. You wouldn't know any of us now. Inez and Irma are married with four children each. Ian is in law school and Ida started at St. Catherine's this fall. Mama and Dad are alone in the house with little Frankie, who's not so little anymore.

I am an old maid of twenty-three, but life has been too busy for settling down as Irma and Inez say I should. I've been abroad and I finally found my vocation, though I guess it really found me years ago. People pay me to write. Aunt Izzy suggested a college for me in California and I lived with her for four years while I went to school. I am a reporter at the *St. Paul Dispatch Pioneer Press* and I've published two short stories in *Women on the Job*. Maybe one day I'll write for the *National Geographic* and see the world. Or perhaps I will write a book about a certain filling station owner.

Mr. Frank has been my dad now longer than you were my Papa on Palace. He was good to me from the start, and I love him most for letting me love you best. And I still do (love you).

Une jeune fille très évoluée (Your girl with an independent attitude),

Isabelle